Epsilon E

SMOKE IN THE SANCTUARY

Stephen Oliver was born in Southampton in 1963. After education at St. Mary's College there, he graduated in Classics from the University of Birmingham and trained as a teacher at Queens' College, Cambridge. He then taught Classics at the Haberdashers' Aske's School, Elstree and the Royal Grammar School, Guildford, before spending a year and a half as a novice monk at Downside Abbey, near Bath. This was followed by four years teaching at Stonyhurst College, Lancashire, where he attained the lofty position of deputy Syntax Playroom Master.

Following six months in the south of France with the Institute of Christ the King, Sovereign Priest, he is now completing an M. Litt. degree in Ancient History at the University of St. Andrews. His interests include ancient Greek religion, cricket, the films of Eric Rohmer and the novels of Anthony Powell. *Smoke in the Sanctuary* is his first novel.

STEPHEN OLIVER

Smoke in the Sanctuary

A novel

Ɛ

Epsilon Books

First published in 2004
by Epsilon Books
31 Rodger Street, Cellardyke, Fife KY10 3HU

Printed in Scotland by West Port Print and Design,
Argyle Street, St. Andrews

A catalogue record for this book is available from the British Library.

ISBN 0-9547120-0-5

FOR MUM AND DAD

---

*From somewhere or other, the smoke of Satan has
entered the sanctuary of the Church.*

Quotation attributed to Pope Paul VI, homily, June 29th,
1972.

L'Abbaye de Notre Dame-de-Monts,
Puissalicon,
France.

July 2nd, 2003.

Dear All,

What on earth am I doing in a monastery in the south of France? That's what you've been asking and that's what I intend to tell you. This may well end up the longest circular letter in history, but I can see no other way of doing justice to the bizarre happenings of the last year. Those of you who aren't Catholics may find the twist and turn of events even harder to grasp, but I shall do my best to make clear why I, an ordinary parish priest and wishing no harm, have had to leave England in something of a hurry.

If it hadn't been for this, I might not now be enjoying the sunshine of the Languedoc in this more than usually sultry July....

Best wishes,
James Page.

(ONE)

I arrived in Cheeseminster, a small, West Country market town, in September of last year to take up my first post as a full-fledged parish priest, filled with optimism and hope despite the rather horrible church that awaited me. Built in the last phase of the ugliest period of the Catholic neo-Gothic revival by one of the least talented exponents of the style, it had unfortunately been untouched by the stray bombs that fell in the area south of Bristol during the war. Successive parish priests, especially from the sixties onwards, had each contributed a little more to its uglification, and on my arrival I noticed that the church had no fewer than three main altars.

The reasons for this didn't take too much working out. The original, admittedly foul, altar would have been deemed too ornate by some priest or other in that revolutionary decade and, in the wake of the changes brought on by the Second Vatican Council, the fiddling would have begun. A leading obsession of the time was, of course, for the priest to have the chance to eye-ball the congregation during Mass, creating the need for a smaller altar from behind which he could do just that. Hence the introduction of altar number two. The third, a kind of wooden table, was, as I later discovered, put there by the last incumbent, a man of the present day liturgical vanguard who considers stone altars highly triumphalist and not at all democratic. It was practically at the level of the congregation, magically eliminating all sense that the celebrant was in any way a man apart. Needless to say, the altar rails had long gone, as had most of the sanctuary furniture. All in all it was as messy an interior as I had seen for a long time.

Cheeseminster itself, however, I liked. A quiet, rather sleepy place, it has been largely unspoilt by the planners and boasts a number of fine municipal buildings, as well as the rather beautiful mediaeval Anglican parish church which doubles as the Minster. There is one other Catholic church, about which more later. I therefore settled down to enjoy my time in the parish, unaware of the clouds that were already looming.

The earliest intimation I had of trouble was at my first Sunday Masses. When I arrived, I found that there were two of these, one at eight o'clock and one at eleven. Not having had time to move it, I said the eight o'clock Mass from behind the wooden altar, but found the whole experience so underwhelming that I decided to lug it off into the sacristy before the eleven o'clock. This wasn't particularly difficult as it was incredibly light, seemingly built of plywood or possibly even cardboard. There was no music at the earlier Mass, and the congregation seemed largely to consist of a few old ladies who enjoyed getting up with the lark. I'd been told that Father Hicks, my modernist predecessor, had wanted to suppress this Mass, on the grounds that to have two Masses on a Sunday was 'divisive', but that the old biddies had complained so much that he had been forced to continue it. My suspicion is that Hicks is a lazy swine who doesn't enjoy keeping early hours, but that may be uncharitable. At any rate, the Mass went ahead, but I later learned that Hicks got his own back by bringing in the cardboard altar at about this time. The biddies had complained again, but had been told by their pastor that the Vatican Council had made specific provision for the introduction of portable altars. Asked why this had never happened before, despite the fact that the Council had ended in

1965, Hicks had lamented the slowness of the people to accept change and the timidity of the priests in charge before him. The biddies had gone off in retreat to consult their liturgical manuals and for a while an uneasy status quo had reigned.

After a hasty breakfast, I had returned to the church to prepare for my eleven o'clock appointment. Despite my early arrival, I was greeted by the sight of a small, rather wizened man in his fifties trying to drag the wooden altar back onto the sanctuary. Despite its portability, he seemed to be having a great deal of trouble and I hurried up to him with the intention of assuring him his efforts were in vain. He, however, managed to get in first.

'Hello, Father,' he said, somewhat tetchily. 'I'm just putting the altar back. Some idiot seems to have moved it.'

He now approached me, wiping his brow with a handkerchief extracted from the pocket of a rather grimy pair of trousers. With a large nose and sparse hair, he did not look in the best of health. His face was pale and his jacket hung from his body as from a scarecrow. He also seemed to have a limp.

'My name's Desmond O'Grady,' he continued. 'I'm in charge of the altar servers here.'

I explained that I was the idiot who had moved the altar.

'Oh, I don't think Miss Phillips would like that,' he said, now looking definitely perturbed. 'You'll have to talk to her before making any changes of that kind.'

'Who is Miss Phillips?'

'Head of the Liturgy Planning Group.'

I recalled that this was another of the innovations my predecessor had brought in, a group of lay people to 'plan' how the various Masses would be celebrated. I informed O'Grady that I would take personal responsibility for the removal of the altar and that he was free to put it back again where he had found it. He did not look convinced.

'Taking the altar away will confuse all the servers, Father. We've just got into the hang of doing things differently and some of the little lads and lasses will be terribly upset if you start changing things again.'

I felt that with this argument he was on stronger ground and had visions of my first big Mass at St. Aelred's being something akin to a rugby scrum. I decided to let him have his way, at least for this week.

'I'll help you put it back then, Mr. O'Grady. I hope you haven't hurt yourself moving it.'

'No, no. Just a little twinge. I'll be all right in a couple of days.'

He didn't sound terribly mollified and it was clear my decision to move the altar without consultation had not made me a new friend in the parish.

When we had finished, a steady stream of altar servers began to arrive, cluttering up the small sacristy and making it difficult for me to vest. The noise was considerable, and O'Grady did his best to make it worse with considerable fussing around a gang of tiny girls whose function was not at first clear. All began to dress in long white garments that made them look like a convention of Moroccan street traders. Eventually, O'Grady managed to get them all into something approximating a line and we staggered into public view to the sound of what appeared to be a thousand guitars and a corps of drums. This, evidently some kind of parish 'folk group', had occupied at least half of one side of the sanctuary. A hyperactive midget was standing in front of them waving his arms while the congregation remained indifferent to the noise, clearly unimpressed by the racket. I recognised the hymn as *God's My Friend*.

God's my friend, He is love, He has risen from above,
Shares my life, shares my woes, knows my head down to my
toes.

This went on for about fifteen verses, and I was left standing at the altar for what seemed like half an hour as the choir worked its way through the whole hymn. I felt like occupying the time by hauling off the wooden altar again, but thought better of it and instead tried to assess the demographic spread of the congregation. Most of them, as I had suspected, were over fifty, but there was a smattering of young families and the odd young, single person, the latter constituency looking least impressed by the noise that was blaring forth from the sanctuary. Eventually the midget had had enough and signalled the choir to stop. This was ignored by the drummer, however, who finished off with a lengthy flourish just as I had opened my mouth to pronounce the Sign of the Cross.

Now, I'm well aware that most of my brother clergy think it indispensable to begin the Mass with some lengthy, impromptu piece of waffle about how nice it is that we should all be meeting again and what joy it is to celebrate the day of the Lord. However, a few years ago I decided to dispense with this, observing that the congregation, despite a show of respectful attention, was not really taking in any of my rather banal ramblings. Furthermore, the Mass was usually quite long enough without me adding my two pennies' worth every five minutes, so we got on with it without further ado, at least until the folk group decided to burst into song again. This they did with the *Gloria*, an irritating version that I had come across before which involved a good deal of clapping and repetition of one or two rather trite phrases. The drummer really let himself go here, as did the midget, who was practically running on the spot in his excitement. This set the pattern for the rest of the Mass, an exhausting experience that left my ear drums shattered and with a feeling that things were going to have to change if I wished to remain in the parish for very long. How, though, I wondered, to achieve this in the teeth of a Liturgy Planning Group and a well-established folk choir?

I began to realise what I was really up against after the Mass when, sailing into view under the porch as I was shaking hands with the departing Mass-goers, came a rather alarming-looking woman in her sixties wearing what looked like a druidic cloak and a turban. She had strong features and a remarkably prominent nose, her eyebrows forming an unbroken arc above some rather glitzy spectacles. This turned out to be Miss Phillips.

'Hello, Miranda Phillips,' she said, shaking my hand rather forcefully.

'James Page.'

'Welcome to the parish, James. We were very sad to see Bill Hicks go, but I'm sure you'll help us build on his remarkable legacy.'

Now, I don't deny that my name is James, but I'm more used to being called Father Page by parishioners. No doubt my modernist predecessor had encouraged the use of first names, but this was not something I felt comfortable with. As for his 'legacy', it remained to be seen whether I wanted to further it.

'Ah, yes, Miss Phillips,' I replied, hoping to sound suitably distant, 'I believe you run the Liturgy Planning Group.'

'Yes, James, and there are one or two things I'd like to pick you up on when we next meet. Today's Mass was far from what we're used to here and I really think you need some educating.'

'Oh.'

I was too shocked to say anything else.

'Yes. Your style is positively antediluvian. Where were you parish priest before?'

'I wasn't. I was an assistant.'

'Well, it shows. You have much to learn.'

Though stunned I decided, for the moment at least, to try to be polite.

'Thank you for being so frank.'

'I haven't started yet.'

She gave me a look evidently designed to chill the blood and I stood, frozen to the spot, as she sailed off in search of another victim. Things were getting worse by the minute, but I didn't have long to contemplate matters. Next to approach was Desmond O'Grady.

12

'Father,' he said, looking as if the world was about to end, 'there are one or two things we'll have to go through together. The little girlies were mighty confused by some of the things you did today. Didn't know whether they were coming or going.'

Once again, I was stumped for a suitable reply.

'It seemed all right to me.'

'Oh, no, not at all. Some of them were in tears afterwards. Could take them weeks to get over it.'

'I'm sorry.'

'Don't worry yourself about it. I'm sure, after a little bit of practice, you'll get the hang of things here.'

'Thanks.'

He limped off, taking a rather unpleasant odour with him, and I hoped that his suit and the dry cleaners would soon be making a much needed acquaintance. I was wondering why the singing midget had not shown up to deliver his credentials when a few minutes later he appeared, clutching at a battered acoustic guitar and beaming from ear to ear. He clearly felt that today's performance had been well up to form.

'Great to meet you, Jim,' he said, rather nasally. 'I thought the guys done really well today.'

'Did you?'

'Oh, yes. Looking forward to seeing you at the Liturgy Planning Group.'

It hadn't crossed my mind that this fellow would turn out to be a stalwart of that particular body too. He now revealed that he was called Greg Tonks and was a minor celebrity in his own right in Cheeseminster, being the moving spirit behind a folk group called the Nurdles. About five feet tall and very hairy, with a greying beard and enormous ears, he certainly looked the part. He now offered to sell me a CD that the folk choir had recently recorded.

'Don't I get one free?' I suggested jokingly. 'Given that I'm your parish priest.'

Tonks looked sourly at me.

'I suppose I could give you one for nothing,' he mused, 'but I'll have to see whether we've broken even yet. For some reason, I've still got a lot to shift.'

He shuffled off, looking distinctly unhappy. I had clearly failed to make a hit with this parishioner either.

After lunch, it struck me as a good idea to spend some time getting the feel of the physical layout of the parish. Essentially, this took in the whole of the centre of Cheeseminster. The church stood in its own, fairly extensive grounds, encompassing the presbytery, a parish hall and a car park, which were situated on one of the roads leading from the market square. I walked up this and found myself facing a large cobbled area and the imposing bulk of the Anglican Minster. One of the more agreeable aspects of my appointment to Cheeseminster was that an old university friend of mine, Spencer White, had recently been installed as vicar there and would be someone to chew the cud with should clerical life become too much. The town hall and library stood on another side of the square, while a number of shops took up the rest of the space. Walking on further, I passed more rows of shops and a number of public houses, before finally finding myself in a more obviously residential district of Victorian and Edwardian cottages. This was no doubt where the bulk of my parishioners lived. Eventually, the older houses gave way to newer ones and I realised I had reached the suburb containing the town's other Catholic church, the Holy Name, a modern structure built at the time the town was expanding in the sixties. I decided to pay a visit on my colleague in the cloth, Father Terry Molloy, possibly the scruffiest priest in the diocese.

'Hello, Terry,' I said as his moth-eaten figure appeared at the door. Now in his fifties, he had once been a rising star in the diocese, but certain problems regarding the bottle had put a stop to all that and he had been shovelled off to these unlovely suburbs. While I, in contrast to many of my colleagues, still favoured the traditional collar and clerical suit, Terry was firmly in the camp of 'let's wear whatever Oxfam

14

are throwing out this week,' not, in Terry's case, necessarily through conviction, merely the expression of a natural untidiness that shuddered at formality. I seemed to have roused him from his afternoon slumbers, for he looked decidedly bleary-eyed as he half-opened the door to see who his visitor was, and what remained of his hair was standing up in large, uncombed tufts above his ears. A cardigan that might recently have been mauled by an angry cat was draped over a check shirt covered in gravy stains, while his trousers, pitted with holes and burn marks, were held up with an old scout belt. He lit up a cigarette as he beckoned me in.

'Sorry I didn't come to the door at once,' he said, between coughs. 'Had a bit too much of the old vino for lunch and fell asleep during *Eastenders*.'

I had visited him at this residence before, and noted again his failure to do anything about the peeling, nicotine-stained wallpaper of the hall and the tottering furniture in the sitting room. The whole house took one straight back to the era when the place had been built, his predecessor having been an old codger who had made as little alteration to the décor as Terry. He now turned off the television and waved me to a seat covered with supplements from that day's *News of the World*.

'How are you enjoying St. Aelred's so far?' he asked.

'Not much,' I replied. 'All the parishioners seem out to get me.'

'Who have you met?'

'Miranda Phillips, Desmond O'Grady and Greg Tonks.'

He shook his head and assumed a grim expression.

'God help you, then. I had the Phillips woman here in this parish until she realised I wasn't about to change anything just because of her say-so. Very thick with the bishop, Miranda, but what she hadn't bargained on was that my star has fallen so low with his lordship that I didn't care what she told him. In the end she went off in a huff and when Hicks arrived at St. Aelred's found herself in her element. You'll

15

have to watch her very carefully, Jim. She took some course or other in liturgy at one of those trendy colleges and has absorbed any amount of mindless junk.'

This sounded so unpromising, I decided to move on.

'What about O'Grady?' I asked.

'More dangerous than he looks. Seems like a shambling fool but somehow or other always manages to get his way.'

'How do you know?'

'The last head altar server at St. Aelred's is now in this parish. There was a sort of coup when Hicks arrived and O'Grady took over from my man.'

This didn't sound any better.

'And Tonks?'

'Don't know him. But I've been forced once or twice to listen to the Nurdles at parish functions here. Do you like West Country folk music, Jim?'

'No.'

'Well, even if you did, you wouldn't like the Nurdles.'

I knew Molloy was a miserable old so-and-so, but was inclined to believe his reading of my parishioners after what I had seen of them myself. I asked him if he thought I would have any allies in the parish.

'Oh, the rank and file are fine, I suppose,' he replied. 'It's just that the loonies have been allowed to take over the shop. Your job is to get some power back.'

'Easier said than done,' I said.

'It'll be your funeral if you don't.'

An hour or so later I returned to the parish, not entirely cheered by what I had heard.

The next great excitement occurred on the Tuesday evening when the Liturgy Planning Group assembled at the presbytery for their first meeting with me. As well as Tonks, O'Grady and Phillips there were three other, rather hangdog people whose names I did not catch and who turned out to say little as the meeting progressed, evidently terrorised by the

16

stronger personalities in the group. Just as we were about to start, the doorbell rang and another woman, of about the same age as Phillips, came in. The two of them greeted each other effusively, as if they were long lost sisters, and I learned that she was the local representative of the We Are Right! group, or WAR! as they are sometimes known. I had read about these people in the Catholic press, a group of laity who spend their time carping about the Vatican and blaming the Pope for all the evils in the world. They style themselves as a 'loyal opposition', but from what I had read the emphasis was on the opposition, not the loyalty. Phillips, after introducing the newcomer as Lavender Buller, told me how delighted I should be to have such a celebrity in the parish, but I merely grunted by way of reply, unable to think of any adequate response. Buller, it was clear, was one of those energetic, forward-thinking pensioners now so rife in the Church, whose ultimate aim is to wrest power from the clergy and generally make a nuisance of themselves. For a moment I was overwhelmed by her rather blousy personality and remembered the dire prophecies made by Terry Molloy. A whiff of some pungent and heavily-applied perfume had begun to fill the room and my attention was immediately drawn by the enormous red bow tied beneath her chin, topping off an expensive-looking jacket of the kind most often seen worn by rich Italian women. Beneath was a pair of rather loud, check trousers and, to complete the assemblage, Buller carried a voluminous handbag with gold clasps. The whole provided a definite contrast to the quasi-religious garb of Phillips, who had once again chosen to wear her druidic costume, though minus the turban. As Buller's perfume continued to permeate the room, I reflected that it had the one advantage of obscuring the unsavoury aroma coming from O'Grady, who had not yet had his appointment with Sketchley's.

'Are you familiar with the work of We Are Right!, James?' asked Phillips.

'Only from what I've read in the Catholic press.'

'Don't believe everything you read there,' said Buller, giving her friend a conspiratorial nod. 'However, *Nuns and Laywomen* were kind enough to print one of my letters earlier this year, attacking the Holy Father for his stance on contraception.'

'How splendid for you.'

'Yes. I think it made an impact.'

'Does the Pope read *Nuns and Laywomen*?'

'I have no idea.'

She gave me a look as if to suggest that flippancy in such an area would not be taken lightly. I found out later that, back in the heady days of the sixties, she had started her career as a radical young nun, later on discarding the veil to become a full-time trouble-maker. In this she operated jointly with her husband, a certain Dr. Bernie Buller, an academic specialising in liturgy. In fact, only the week before I had read an article of his in *Liturgy Update* on the subject of kneeling in church. I mentioned this now.

'Oh, yes?' she said, as if this was only to be expected. 'Well, I'm sorry, but my husband won't be here tonight. He has to address an interfaith group at the university on the subject of sex before marriage.'

'How interesting.' I said. 'Is he for or against?'

Once again, she gave me a look as if to suggest that I should take care not to speak lightly of holy things and then settled down into the only remaining chair. The sitting-room of the presbytery was not large, but I was now told that my modernist predecessor had been in the habit of providing supper for them all and I was asked if I intended to continue the practice.

'I shouldn't think so. I'm a terrible cook.'

'Oh, but we can help,' piped up a mousy woman in the corner, who seemed to have been fired into life by this mention of food. 'I'm sure Margaret and I could give you a hand.'

Margaret turned out to be another mousy woman on her left.

'I can bring a bit of scrumpy,' said Tonks, also animated by a turn towards gastronomic matters.

'Well, we'll see,' I said. 'Perhaps it could be done. I'll think about it.'

This wasn't good enough for Phillips.

'Oh, stop beating about the bush, James. Are we going to have food here next time or aren't we? I think we should vote on it.'

I thought this was a bit much, given that I was the one whose kitchen was going to be used and who would probably end up doing the bulk of the cooking, with or without the help of the mousy women, but I let the vote go ahead. This resulted in a unanimous decision that food should be provided, so I was evidently stuck with it. Phillips, as chairperson, now took control of the meeting and distributed an agenda. Not surprisingly, the first thing to come up was the previous Sunday's Masses. Tonks was thanked for the 'truly wonderful music' provided by his gang of hillbillies, with special praise going for a tune he had written himself and which had been played after Communion. This to me had sounded like a commercial for washing powder, but I let it go. After various other contributors had also been praised, including the readers, altar servers and 'welcomers', Phillips now turned her attention to me.

'Well, James,' she said, looking rather arch, 'how did *you* feel the Mass went.'

This was rather a difficult question. How critical should I be? I had loathed just about everything to do with it, but decided I should restrict my comments to one or two small points this time round and broaden my attack at future meetings. However, I now realised that Phillips's question had actually been rhetorical, for she quickly continued with 'because I have one or two things to say about your own contribution.'

'Oh, yes?' I said, warily.

'Yes, indeed. Now, you are, of course, new to the parish and, if I may say so, still quite inexperienced in the

19

ways of the diocese. I believe you were only ordained four years ago.'

I admitted that this was so and that I had previously been an accountant.

'I see. Well, many of us here have a wide experience of the liturgy and have attended courses at the pastoral centre. I am sure you would like to profit from our knowledge.'

She gave me a smile of pure malice, as if anticipating the enjoyment she would derive from the next few minutes.

'Fire away,' I said, nervously.

I braced myself for the attack. There was a hush in the room and I sensed that the other members of the group were also looking forward to hearing the ticking-off that was coming my way.

'First of all, please explain why did you not give a speech of welcome at the beginning of the Mass.'

I did so at some length but clearly failed to satisfy Phillips, who made a tutting sound when I had finished.

'I think you must be the only priest in the diocese who is of that opinion,' she moaned. 'Going straight into the Mass without a speech of welcome can only be construed as a hostile act. I am sure the people were most upset. I sensed it very strongly. Then there is your failure to clap during the *Gloria*.'

'I hate clapping in church.'

There was a sharp intake of breath at this from practically the whole group and Tonks even went so far as to break into a fit of coughing.

'And on what grounds do you make this objection?'

This was from Buller, who sounded, if anything, even more hostile than her friend.

'It doesn't seem very reverent.'

It was a few moments before anyone said anything.

'I think, James,' remarked Phillips, 'that you are locked into an outmoded concept of what constitutes Church.'

There were many nodding heads around the room, but I found myself reflecting more on her irritating refusal to say '*the* Church', dropping the article clearly being a piece of trendy newspeak that she had picked up at the pastoral centre.

'I disagree,' I said.

It was now Buller's turn again.

'When was the last time you attended one of Father Mack's liturgy refresher courses, James?' she asked.

'I have never attended one of Father Mack's liturgy refresher courses.'

'Impossible! I will give you his telephone number straight after this meeting. It evidently won't be soon enough for you.'

After a few more brickbats had been thrown my way, the meeting moved on to the thorny question of something called 'the baptismal pool'. I wasn't completely unprepared for this as, in my idler moments, I occasionally read various church furnishing magazines and knew that baptismal pools were all the rage. Apparently, advanced liturgists in the United States had taken a few moments off from trimming their beards to decide that the Rite of Baptism was infinitely more 'authentic' if carried out in a full-scale pool rather than over a traditional font. As a result, no church reordering was now complete without an enormous pool being situated somewhere near the porch. I therefore had my contribution to this topic ready.

'Oh, I don't really think that we can start considering a baptismal pool now,' I said. 'When, in a few years time, we are ready to ponder a thoroughgoing reordering of the church, we can examine the question then.'

Knowing the predilection in the modern Church for re-jigging church interiors every few years to reflect the latest thinking from advanced Americans, I had thought this answer up to forestall any discussion of baptismal pools and the like. However, as usual Buller and Phillips were ahead of me.

'I'm glad you brought that up,' said the former, rather smugly, while drawing some kind of document folder out of her outsize handbag. 'As you can see, plans for the reordering

21

are next on the agenda. They were well advanced just before Bill's move.'

This caught me on the wrong foot, for I hadn't had time to take in the agenda properly and had not noticed that reordering was on the menu. No one at Bishop's House, and least of all Hicks himself, had mentioned anything about it. Buller now distributed copies of the plan.

'Most of you have seen a draft of this, of course, but clearly Bill hasn't bothered to tell you, James. How remiss of him.'

I already smelled a rat. The whole thing was no doubt a set-up, a collusion between Hicks and the Liturgy Group to ensure that I was unprepared for discussion on the issue and therefore easily bounced into agreeing to the whole thing. Was the diocesan machinery in on this too? If so, someone quite high up clearly hated my guts and had foreseen that I might not be entirely in sympathy with the proposals. Perhaps Hicks had been nervous that his wonderful plans would fall with his departure and wanted to ensure that someone he no doubt viewed as a dangerous reactionary like me could not scupper them. How did they know what I felt on matters of this kind? At the seminary and afterwards I had been very careful to keep my views to myself and I thought I had emerged as the ultimate fence-sitter on all important issues. Clearly this was where I had gone wrong. Nothing short of wholehearted approval for the liturgical revolution was going to be enough for these people. I examined my copy of the proposals and saw that all the latest fetishes were there: removal of the old high altar, reorientation of the church, extensive carpeting, new entrance hall (or 'greeting area') and, of course, the pool.

'But this will cost thousands,' I said.

'Oh, don't worry about that, Jim,' said Tonks. 'It's all been costed. Isn't that right, Desmond?'

It turned out that O'Grady was the parish's Director of Finance and that he, along with Hicks, had had intensive discussions with the arm of the diocesan bureaucracy that dealt with this sort of thing. There was still quite a bit of money to be raised, he said, but an appeal would take care of that. I decided to try and buy some time.

'Surely it would be more appropriate to discuss all this at the Parish Council?' I said, rather desperately.

'Of course, James, of course,' said Phillips. 'It's coming up at the next meeting. However, tonight we can begin to plan how our approach to the liturgy will have to change to reflect the new orientation of the church. I'm sure, for instance, that Desmond will have much to say about the opportunities it will afford his servers for greater and more active participation in the liturgy.'

O'Grady looked slightly less enthusiastic about this than about the more general proposals, and I wondered whether he was already foreseeing trouble in getting his 'girlies' to adapt to further changes. There now began a general and rather high-flown discussion about how everything would change for the better in the brave new world of the reordered church, the quieter members of the group nodding furiously whenever Buller or Phillips uttered some up-to-the-minute liturgical buzzword. I, meanwhile, kept my head down, realising that for this meeting at least there was nothing further I could say. Eventually they all took their leave and I settled down to a can of beer in front of the television.

It was clearly going to be a long, hard battle.

(TWO)

My next move, I decided, would need to be a serious chat with Terry Molloy, the only man I knew who was bloody-minded enough to have any idea what to do in a perilous situation like this. Of course, I was aware that these reordering schemes were all the rage in the diocese, not to mention the Church at large, but I had somehow felt that the moment would not come for me to confront one quite so soon in my career as a PP. Furthermore, until then I had not really given the matter as a whole much thought and it was only now that I tried to rationalise my gut feelings against the scheme. Why exactly did I feel so opposed to the plan? What was wrong with a baptismal pool and an altar in the middle of the church? If I were going to make serious objections to the scheme, I would have to do better than just say I didn't like them. I would have to give reasons. No doubt the deadly duo of Phillips and Buller could quote endless reams of spurious nonsense from right-on books and periodicals that advocated just such a reversal of all that was familiar and tried in the Church, so I would need to come up with some equally authoritative sources against. I was certain, from my admittedly limited reading on the subject, that such sources existed: I would simply have to locate them and read up on them as fast as possible. Before telephoning Terry I therefore decided to put a search out on the internet for liturgical books, and eventually ran to ground two that looked promising, one by an Austrian Vatican official named Cardinal Schmidt and another by the renowned liturgical historian, Monsignor O'Shea. Having ordered these, I picked up the phone.

'Terry?' I said.

'Jim. What, more problems already?'

I explained the situation and there was a pause.

'Congratulations,' he said. 'You have reached the crossroads of your career.'

I had no idea what he was talking about.

'Already?' I said.

'Yep. What you do in the next week will decide the whole future orientation of your life. You can either opt for an easy, placid existence, probably ending up in a bishopric with plaudits all the way from the liberal establishment, or …'

Another pause.

'Yes?'

'… a life of confrontation and, in the end, exile or banishment.'

I found this pretty hard to believe.

'Is it really as stark as that?' I said.

'Yes.'

'Why, what will I be up against if I decide to oppose the plans for the reordering?'

It took him about half an hour to explain it to me, but eventually I got the picture. He described the diocese as I had never imagined it, outlining a scenario I had seen glimpses of but the full import of which I had never guessed. It was a tale of power concentrated in the hands of a bureaucracy as able to make or break a priest as one of the old communist politburos of the cold war. Was I to believe him or had he been drinking? I knew that Terry's career had gone off the rails and that there were some who described him as a twisted and embittered figure, but if he were right I would be gambling everything if I decided to oppose Buller, Phillips and their ilk.

'They're all in it together, old son,' he explained. 'It's an establishment with its origins right back in the sixties. The bishop, of course, is too scared to do anything, and anyway he half believes all that guff about the spirit of Vatican Two and the need for endless change. The rest of them are true believers. If I were you I'd have a word with Canon Taylor.'

'What, the old codger out at Muckford?'

'Yes.'

'But he must be about ninety-three.'

'That may be so, but he's still got all his marbles. He was ordained for the diocese about seventy years ago and has seen everything. He objected to the new Mass when it came out and they shuffled him off to that loony-bin at Muckford. However, as I say, he's as sane as you or me – saner, probably. Go and see him if you don't believe what I've told you.'

I tried to get my head round all this. I had, of course, been only a small boy when the new Mass came in after the Council so knew little of the controversies of the period. All I really knew was that a few old stagers like the canon had been allowed to continue saying the traditional Mass, so long as they didn't do it in public. I told Terry that I might take up his suggestion and go and see the old fellow, but privately wondered if there was any point. What I needed was tactical, strategic advice, and at the moment I wasn't getting any.

I put down the phone and decided to forget about the whole business of the reordering and go and pay my respects to the head teacher of St. Aelred's primary school, just across the road from the presbytery. She had invited me to sit in on a few Religious Education lessons and to make the acquaintance of some of the teachers and pupils, an invitation I had willingly accepted after the rumpus of my first few days in the parish. Perhaps here, in confronting the innocence of youth, I might be able to regain some optimism about my appointment. Furthermore, I had agreed to say Mass for the children in the school hall and was greatly looking forward to being able to do so without the presence of Tonks and his cronies.

On my arrival I was introduced to a Miss Anderson, who was in charge of one of the more senior classes. Now, it is a well known fact that a man must accept a life of holy celibacy on embracing the Catholic priesthood, and since my ordination I had so far not had too much trouble putting the stirrings of the flesh behind me. However, if anyone was going to keep me awake at night with thoughts of what I had left behind, it was Miss Anderson. About twenty-five, wearing a low-cut dress and highly curvaceous with it, she was the most attractive primary school teacher I had ever seen. On being introduced to her I studiously avoided taking in too many of her ample attractions and tired to concentrate on the content of the lesson that had just begun. It wasn't long before I had other things on my mind than Miss Anderson's good looks.

The textbook she was using was one I had recently seen panned for watering down Catholic doctrine. In fact, it was widely considered to be the worst Catholic Religious Education textbook currently available. However, I wasn't entirely surprised that the school was using it. I knew that, despite its reputation for heterodoxy, it was in fact extremely popular with the people who ran the influential diocesan education departments. It was called *Look At Me, Lord* and was full of pictures of animals and flowers, the point being to express the 'wonder of God's creation.' The questions it contained were along the lines of 'the Church invites us to come together on Sunday and celebrate our love for one another – What do you think about that?' and, in fact, Miss Anderson had been addressing this very issue as I came in. A rather disturbed-looking boy sitting in the front row with ginger hair and freckles put his hand up to answer the question.

'Does that mean,' he said, wiping his nose with the back of his hand, 'that we can have sex?'

A titter went round the class, and the boy gave me a look as if to say 'Welcome to the lion's den, padre.' I thought, however, that his question was rather a good one, given the woolly language of the textbook.

'No, Warren,' said Miss Anderson, blushing slightly and looking briefly at me before answering the question. 'When we talk about celebrating our love for one another, we don't just mean the kind of love you're talking about. We can love each other as friends as well.'

The class looked sceptical.

'Well, what's that got to do with God, then?' said the boy, clearly not satisfied.

I decided to butt in at this point.

27

'What the book means,' I said, 'Is that we have to go to Mass on Sundays.'

It seemed important to make that clear.

'Well, *I* don't go,' said the boy, giving another wipe of his face. ' I mean, why do something boring like that when you could be down the shops with your mates?'

'So that is what you feel is it, Warren?' said Miss Anderson.

'Yes, Miss.'

'Does anyone else have any thoughts about this?'

A girl at the back, who had been fidgeting throughout this exchange, stuck up her hand.

'Yes, Kaylie? What do you think?'

'Nothing, Miss. Can I go to the toilet?'

Things continued in this desultory fashion for another ten minutes or so, various trouble-makers continuing to try to bring the discussion back to more steamy questions. Miss Anderson coped with it all pretty well, but by the end of the lesson I felt that the kiddies had learnt precisely zero about Church teaching on anything. I put this to her in the corridor afterwards.

'Oh, it doesn't do to be too dogmatic,' she said. 'The course-book is quite firm about that. They have to discover these things from their own experience. Why, what's the use of a faith that you just learn by rote? All that went out with the ark.'

The subject was such a large one and she was obviously busy, so I let it go. Furthermore I had to prepare for the Mass and so made my excuses and headed for the assembly hall. This, like the rest of the school, was a modern structure and doubled as a gym. Eventually the children filed in and I was presented with a couple of altar servers. The headmistress told me that I was not to fear and that plenty of music had been prepared, as well as a dramatic reconstruction of the Gospel. This was not what I had hoped for. Fortunately, however, no drums were in evidence and only one guitar. The children sang quite nicely, but whoever was in charge had obviously rifled through *Hymns New and Newer* and come up with the most infantile pap she could find. We had a couple of verses of *God Loves Me, He Loves My Bear*, and I suddenly noticed that all the children were clutching small, furry stuffed animals.

Yes, it was my worst nightmare, a teddy bear Mass! I had seen one of these while on holiday in the States, but couldn't believe that they had already reached these shores. The little choir sang with gusto:

> *God loves me, He loves my bear,*
> *Wherever I go, He's always there.*
> *We say a prayer in bed at night,*
> *And when we wake it's morning light.*

It was all a long way from *Soul of My Saviour* and the hymns of my youth. However, this was nothing compared to the acting-out of the gospel, which that day concerned the return of the prodigal son. No sooner had I started reading it when a couple of children dressed as pigs were ushered forward and there was much toing and froing as the prodigal son was seen to work in a pig-sty. We then had a rather dramatic representation of a cow being slaughtered for the feast, though one of the teachers explained afterwards that cows didn't feel anything when they died, something I'm not sure some of the younger children believed. I kept my homily as short as possible and was relieved when it was all over and I could get back to the presbytery.

How to get rid of *Look at Me, Lord* and replace it with *Dogma and Doctrine*, my textbook of choice? That was the thought uppermost in my mind as I ate an uneasy lunch and began to ponder ways of bringing such much needed changes about.

(THREE)

In due course my liturgy books arrived and in what spare moments I had I devoured them with relish. They were exactly what I'd been after. The authors both put an extremely cogent case for tradition and showed convincingly, to my mind, that there was no need at all for the kind of changes the liturgy group had been proposing. Such notions as baptismal pools and altars half-way up the church were, quite simply, what I'd thought they were – fads dreamed up by loony academics determined to justify their salaries in some third rate mid-western college. It was on this sort of stuff that the diocesan bureaucracies fed, Terry had explained, in order to give them a reason for existing. If you convince enough people that constant change is necessary than everyone is kept busy and the salaries keep rolling in. Furthermore, some of them no doubt actually believed in all this stuff and really felt that what the Church needed was a bit of democracy in the assembly, a place where we 'celebrated ourselves as community,' to use the jargon, and put God firmly on the back-burner. Well, Monsignor O'Shea and Cardinal Schmidt were having none of it and I now had the ammunition I needed to show the Bullers of this world that their ideas were as crackpot as they were expensive. I wondered what the ordinary parishioner thought of it all, though judging by the steep fall in Mass attendance figures over the last thirty years the answer was staring me in the face. I began to speculate what would happen if I started a counter-attack and remembered Terry's comments about exile and banishment. Nevertheless, perhaps it was worth a try. Of one thing I was sure – I didn't want the reordering.

As I was musing on all this after a hasty breakfast, the doorbell rang and I opened up to find myself in the presence of a thin and intense-looking young man who had been part of the Mass congregation that morning. It was a

Wednesday and I had instigated a seven-thirty Mass for people who wanted one before going to work. The attendance had not been enormous, but there seemed to be enough interest to continue the experiment and I kept the plywood altar well out of the way. Fortunately, no members of the Liturgy Planning Group had so far seen fit to attend a weekday Mass and I had been spared any further criticisms of my methodology.

'Hello, Father,' said my visitor. 'Do you mind if I come in? There's something I'd like to talk to you about.'

I remembered now that this person had also been to confession that week and was clearly a pretty regular communicant. As he spoke, he rubbed his hands and looked rather pained, his shirt not looking adequate protection against the cool September day. He was wearing large, square spectacles that didn't really suit him and his clothes seemed made for another person, so untidily did they hang from his spare frame. Although clearly only in his early twenties, he was already losing his hair and there was an unhealthy pallor to his face as if he spent all his time indoors. As he came in he explained that his name was Mark Spooner and that he was a doctoral engineering student at the nearby University of the Levels, a fourth rate institution if ever there was one. I asked him to sit down.

'It's like this, Father,' he said, screwing up his eyes and giving his hands an extra rub. 'I need your advice.'

'Go on, then.'

At this point he seemed reluctant to continue, so I gave him my best reassuring smile and, after stammering over the first syllables a little, he gradually became more fluent.

'I hope I am not about to shock you, Father.'

'Oh, you can't shock me,' I replied, trying to sound reassuring. 'I've heard it all.'

'I bet you haven't heard this.'

'Try me.'

I wished he'd get to the point as I was due over at the school fairly soon and wanted to do some paperwork before setting off. Finally, it all came out in a rush.

'It's to do with girls, Father,' he stammered. 'You see, I don't have a great deal of luck in that area and a few weeks ago I thought I might try the ICDA.'

'The what?'

'The Internet Catholic Dating Agency.'

'Well,' I said, trying to sound encouraging, 'that seems like a good idea.'

He looked far from convinced.

'I'm not so sure.'

He now gave me a blow by blow account of his experiences with this organisation, evidently set up to help poor saps like himself find a like-minded girlfriend. It turned out that he had managed to start an on-line conversation with a woman called Deirdre, who seemed at first to have the credentials he was looking for but unfortunately hadn't provided a photograph.

'Do you think looks are important in a relationship, Father?'

'Well, yes, I do,' I said. 'There has to be an element of physical attraction for the relationship to work.'

'That's what I'm now beginning to think. When I first met Deirdre she turned out to be hideously ugly.'

He paused and I wondered whether I was expected to say something.

'Isn't that a little unfair?' I ventured. 'After all, beauty is, as they say, in the eye of the beholder.'

'I'd like to meet a beholder who would have found Deirdre beautiful.'

He paused again, clearly conjuring up an image of the girl's lack of pulchritude and visibly shuddering as he did so. I thought it time we moved on.

'Did you go out together at all?'

'Yes, we did. We went to the cinema.'

'And how did the evening go?'

I could read from his expression that the report was not going to be a favourable one.

32

'Not very well,' he stammered. 'I'm told it isn't good to see a film on a first date. You don't get much chance to talk and it takes up most of the evening. I was quite glad it was dark, though, as it meant I didn't have to look at her face. By the way, I have a picture here which she gave me that evening.'

He passed it over and I was forced to conclude that, if I'd been in his position, I might also have favoured darkness.

'Did you see her again?'

Spooner's face went a shade redder.

'You'll think I'm a fool, Father, but I thought that I might gradually get used to Deirdre's looks, so decided to invite her for a drink in the Frog and Ferret. The evening turned out to be a complete disaster. I discovered she was boring as well as ugly and spent all her time talking about her job. To fill up the time I drank too much beer and by closing-time I was pretty drunk.'

I began to wonder the point of these ramblings and why he had felt it necessary to unburden himself to a priest on the subject. The reason became clear when I asked him what had happened next.

'This is the bit I really need your advice on, Father. You see, she now asked me back to her place, and because I was drunk I accepted. When we got there I started to kiss her.'

He looked at me now as if the remembrance of it was making him feel ill.

'Exactly how drunk were you?'

'Very. In fact, so drunk that I had completely forgotten that I didn't find her attractive. The next thing I knew we were in bed together.'

I wondered, if he was about to tell me had committed some terrible sin with the woman, why he hadn't revealed the gory details in confession. However, as it turned out, and despite Deirdre's evident enthusiasm for things to go further, he had had enough self-control to extricate himself from the situation, make his excuses and leave the house at high speed. Since then, he had been bombarded with calls from his inamorata and had had to get a block put on his mobile phone. He now asked for my opinion of what he had done.

'Well,' I said, trying to weigh it all up. 'First of all, I suggest you control your drinking. If you're bored with someone's conversation in future, try getting through it on soft drinks instead. Are you prone, when you've had a couple, to making physical advances on women you scarcely know and for whom you feel no desire?'

'I don't know, Father. I've never been in this position before.'

'Well, try not to get into it again.'

Spooner began to rub his hands together again and stared morosely at the floor. I didn't want to discourage him too much as he was obviously somewhat immature and completely lacking in self-confidence, so I made some encouraging noises about hoping things would go better the next time.

'I'm not sure if there's going to be a next time,' he said, despondently. 'Do you really think I should try again?'

'I don't see why not. Just because the first woman out of the hat turned out to be a dud doesn't damn all the Catholic women out there. Why not give it another go and come back and tell me how you get on?'

He brightened considerably at this, and when he finally sloped back to the university I decided I was glad he had felt able to confide in me. At least this was real pastoral work, unlike the petty battles that had dominated my time in the parish so far. I looked forward to hearing more of the adventures of this reluctant Don Juan.

FOUR

The more I read the Revd. Messrs. Schmidt and O'Shea, the more emboldened I felt to take on the Liturgy Planning Group when it next met. However, I also concluded that a visit to old Canon Taylor at Muckford wouldn't do me any harm in the battle against the forces of disorder, and therefore decided to drive up to this little village north of Cheeseminster and beard the superannuated fellow in his den. Terry had described the place as a lunatic asylum, but it was of course simply a retirement home for priests run by an equally aged group of nuns. The canon had just finished saying Mass when I arrived.

'Who are you?' he said, in a frail but decidedly firm voice.

'I telephoned to you the other day, Canon,' I replied. 'I'm the parish priest at Cheeseminster.'

'What? Hicks?'

'No. He's my predecessor. I only arrived a few weeks ago.'

'Good,' he said, rather testily. 'I didn't like what I heard about Hicks. The fellow sounds like an out and out modernist.'

'He is, Canon.'

He began to look very angry.

'And how about you?' he said. 'All my brother priests these days seem to have the most extraordinary ideas. I suppose you're no different.'

I expressed the hope that he wouldn't find my ideas too ghastly and he waved me into a rather comfortable sitting-room where a nun was depositing a pot of tea.

'I suppose you'll drink some of this?'

'Thank you.'

I outlined to him my problems and said that I had come to seek his advice at the suggestion of Father Molloy.

35

'Shame about Molloy,' he said. 'He was my assistant for a while at Mickleborough. Very good at first, but he had some kind of crisis over a woman. Took to the bottle and now dresses like a tramp. Do you know him?'

'Yes. As I said, he was the one who advised me to come and see you.'

I felt this was going to be rather hard work, but after sipping at his tea he seemed to wake up a bit and began to tell me about the difficulties in his last parish.

'They brought that new Mass in, you see,' he said, his brows darkening at the scandal of it all. 'Must have been about 1970. Of course, they'd been mucking about with the old Mass for years before that, cutting little bits out and bringing in lots of English. I did my best to fight it, but the advance was remorseless. When the new Mass came in everyone had got used to something ghastly and so accepted it. I tried to keep it dignified, but in the end it was all too much and they packed me off to this place to be chaplain. I got permission to say the old Mass in private.'

He slurped at his tea, looking thoroughly fed up at the thought of what he had been through.

'So what's your problem, then?' he now asked, not looking particularly interested.

I explained in more detail what had been happening.

'I thought it would come to something like this in the end,' he mused, crunching on a biscuit. 'The steamroller was unstoppable. Once you allow the idea of reform, everything unravels. I pity you young priests today. If you want to fight the monstrous horde of laywomen and committeemen who've taken over, you haven't got a chance. You could try, but it'll all end in tears.'

He paused, more despondent than ever, and I outlined the reading I had done on the subject of the Mass and asked him if he knew the books. This was where the meeting really took off. The Canon now revealed that in the dim and distant past he had been the diocesan liturgy expert himself, and had contributed a great deal to publications on the subject, as well as keeping up with things since his retirement. He was evidently pleased at how seriously I was taking liturgical matters and said I should call again if I felt there was anything he could do to help. At this, an idea struck me.

'Would you be prepared,' I said, 'to come to the parish and give a talk?'

'On what?'

'The Mass. Explain why people like Schmidt and O'Shea are right. It might help me to get some of the parishioners on my side.'

He mused for a while and I wondered whether I had gone too far. Perhaps it was even unfair to ask a ninety-three year old man to drag his creaking bones down to Cheeseminster and become involved in my war. However, in the end he replied rather enthusiastically and I felt that he had been pleased to be asked. We fixed a date and I said I would publicise the talk as widely as possible. When I left we shook hands warmly, and he expressed his pleasure that I should have taken the trouble come and see him. The nuns, he said, were all right, but they were no substitute for male company and could never be persuaded to accompany him down to the local pub.

On my return to the parish I really began to get moving, impelled now by a sense of mission. Schmidt and O'Shea had convinced me of two things very quickly. Firstly, that the traditional and authentic way to say the Mass was with one's back to the people, that is, facing the same way as the congregation. At first this had seemed a strange proposition, given that the modern orthodoxy was that the priest should face the congregation so as to have constant eye-contact with them, the theory being that he could then be more 'welcoming' and establish a sort of mystic bond with his fellow worshippers as they partook of the eucharistic meal. However, according to my new gurus, this practice was essentially an invention of the sixties and had no precedent in church history up to that point, apart from some spurious arguments based on the way certain basilicas had been orientated in Rome in the early Christian era. The majority of congregations had, in fact, faced east together with their priests in anticipation of the second coming of Christ, expected to come from that direction. Hence, the priest was not deliberately turning his back on the people so as to ignore them but to lead worship eastwards. I knew that there were one or two churches in England where this still happened, but the vast majority of priests had succumbed to the liturgical winds blowing from the continent and had swiftly erected a new altar in front of the old to enable them to say Mass facing the mob. The old altars had then either been destroyed or rendered redundant.

The second proposition of which I was now convinced was that the Vatican Council had never for a moment intended that Latin should be suppressed as the liturgical language of the Catholic Church. In fact, the documents expressed an ardent desire that Latin should be retained, but once again the vagaries of fashion had decreed that the vernacular should take over and, sheep-like, the vast majority of priests had gone with the trend. The new Mass had, of course, been promulgated in Latin, but few were the parishes where this edition was actually used.

Not for one second while training for the priesthood in the diocesan seminary had I been acquainted with the notions I have outlined above. A little more research showed me that Schmidt and O'Shea were not making these ideas up and once persuaded by their arguments I felt pretty indignant that I had had the wool pulled over my eyes for so long. Had my teachers deliberately kept these facts from me or were they also ignorant of the situation as it really stood? I was inclined to suspect the former, knowing how an agenda can swiftly sideline facts it finds inconvenient to its purposes. My indignation now began to take practical form and for several days I pondered how to do something in the parish that would return worship to a more traditional form and one that would be in fact much closer to that really intended by the Council. Reflecting on Canon Taylor's offer to give a talk on the

38

liturgy, it struck me that I could incorporate this into a series of conferences delivered by me and perhaps others on the same topic, as a way of smoothing the path to any changes I might eventually bring in. I knew that it would only be inviting trouble to make changes without consultation, and it was clearly going to be important to take the parishioners with me as a way of countering the influence of the Liturgy Planning Group. A shudder of fear passed through me as I reflected on the likely rumpus that even the slightest change in a more traditional direction would bring, and I resolved there and then to say a decade of the Rosary every morning for the success of my endeavours.

The fruits of these prayers were swifter in coming than I had hoped. The day after I began them a call from Miranda Phillips revealed that she and Buller were accompanying the latter's husband to a We Are Right! conference somewhere in Wales the following week, and the next meeting of the Liturgy Planning Group would have to be put off. I expressed my regrets at this postponement of one of the chief joys of my schedule, and on putting down the phone decided at once to replace the meeting with a conference of my own on the liturgy. I could then introduce my leading ideas and actually put some of them into action before the wretched women returned. Faced with a *fait accompli*, they might find it very difficult to bring back the status quo afterwards. I knew that they were departing on a Saturday, so decided to announce the talk at the Sunday Masses and deliver it the following Wednesday. The changes would be introduced at the Thursday morning Mass.

There was only one problem in all this: the Latin. I had studied Latin at school for a number of years so could at least understand the language well enough for the purposes of saying Mass. However, I had no idea where I could get hold of a Latin edition of the Mass and, furthermore, was worried that when the time came to say it I would pronounce it so bizarrely that the exercise would become a farce. It rapidly became clear that another visit to the retirement home in Muckford was required, so I drove out again and outlined my plans to Canon Taylor. While commenting on my foolhardiness in taking on the liberal establishment in this way, he was evidently enthused by my radical agenda and swiftly began instruction in the pronunciation of ecclesiastical Latin. He also furnished me with the books required, of which there was a large store at Muckford that the nuns had collected over the years for ageing priests like himself who wanted to use the ancient tongue, whether in the old or the new rite. Armed with these, I returned to Cheeseminster and hastily produced some leaflets to accompany my talk, as well as others for the Mass itself.

When Wednesday evening came round, about thirty people turned up and I spoke for an hour or so before taking questions. Of the Liturgy Planning Group, O'Grady and the two mousy women made an appearance, but there was no sign of Tonks, who apparently had a Nurdles gig at the Frog and Ferret. I decided that I liked the Mice, as I now thought of them, for they were always keen to help with the serving of refreshments and fell into the bracket of those who called me 'Father' and not 'James' or 'Jim'. Furthermore, they never said anything that suggested they had been on a liturgy training course, and I began to wonder whether they could eventually be groomed as future allies in the Fight. O'Grady, meanwhile, only ever appeared to be bothered about how things would work from the servers' point of view, and wider liturgical questions largely passed him by. When I announced that I was planning to introduce a regular Latin Mass every Thursday morning in place of the vernacular Mass currently in place, he immediately questioned me as to how I could possibly expect his 'lads' and 'girlies' to make responses in a dead language. I had anticipated this objection and remarked that it would scarcely make any difference since no server had ever been known to show his face for the weekday Masses anyway. This seemed to disgruntle O'Grady, who muttered something about 'personnel issues', and I was certain that he would be on the phone moaning to Buller and Phillips the moment they got back. Miss Anderson was there, looking as lovely as ever, but she annoyed me at once with some fatuous remarks about how foolish it was to expect modern people to worship in Latin since, unlike me, they wouldn't understand a word of it. I pointed out that I would be providing leaflets including a parallel translation of the Latin into English and, furthermore, that the Reading and the Gospel would be read in English. This seemed to placate her a little and I was pleased that there were no further comments of this type. One or two people expressed their amazement that they had never heard anything like my views before, and I received the impression that an hour's talk would not be enough to convince them that the entire liturgical revolution of the last thirty years had been misguided. However, I had not necessarily expected instant success, and that was why I needed Canon Taylor and some other guns to come in later on my side.

At the end of the meeting, as I was helping the Mice clear up the tea things, I suddenly felt a presence behind me and turned to see a dapper, rather emaciated-looking man standing there as if he would like a word. Balding, he had opted for a Bobby Charlton solution to the problem and several strands of hair had been trained over his thinning dome. He was dressed in an immaculate but rather ancient suit and was scratching his forehead rather nervously as if not sure that the impending conversation was a good idea. I had never seen him before that evening and he had sat quietly at the back during the talk, not taking part in the question and answer session afterwards. It had crossed my mind in a more paranoid moment that he might be some kind of spy sent by the diocesan bureaucracy, but the truth turned out to be quite different.

'Hello, Father Page,' he said, 'I wonder if I might introduce myself. My name is Hubert Drone and I am the diocesan secretary of the CRC.'

We shook hands rather formally and I searched my mind for what the initials stood for.

'CRC?'

'The Campaign for Real Catholicism. Rather like the Campaign for Real Ale, only less alcoholic.'

I later learned that this was the closest Drone ever came to a joke, and he certainly never permitted himself a smile. He now stood there looking at me rather dolefully, as if all should be clear.

'What exactly do you do, Mr. Drone?' I asked, still not really any the wiser.

The enquiry had evidently pleased him, for he now became animated.

'We campaign to bring the Church back to what it was before all the changes were introduced. That is why I came tonight. One of our members tipped me off that you were going to talk about the liturgy and it's been noticed that you removed the wooden altar at the eight o'clock Mass. We thought you might turn out to be on our side.'

I found all this decidedly disturbing, unaware that I was being watched so closely. It was if I had suddenly stepped into a John Le Carré novel.

'Well, Mr. Drone,' I asked. 'Do I pass the test?'

'Oh, yes, I was delighted by your talk. The members of the CRC speak of nothing else but Cardinal Schmidt and Monsignor O'Shea. We are very committed to the concept of the eastwards facing Mass and the use of Latin. Of course, what we really want is the reintroduction of the old rite, but that is proving rather difficult.'

This seemed the understatement of the century, but a gleam had appeared in his eye and I did not want to disillusion the poor fellow. I told him of my acquaintance with Canon Taylor.

'Ah, a wonderful old man and a very holy priest,' he said. 'The bishop permits us to have one old rite Mass a month, and it is Canon Taylor who says it for us at Muckford. Goodness knows what will happen when he eventually dies since very few priests in this diocese either have the time or the inclination to say these Masses. However, I'm delighted that you should at least be introducing your own little venture and shall make every effort to assist.'

He sloped off, not exactly full of the joys of spring but apparently as cheerful as could reasonably be expected. As I emerged from the hall and began to lock up I noticed that Mark Spooner was standing in the darkness of the car park not far off, moodily smoking a cigarette and looking as if the weight of the world was upon him. I asked him how he was, but he did not reply to this, merely asking in an anxious tone of voice, 'have you got a minute, Father?'

My heart sank. It was already late and I still had a few things to prepare for Mass the following day. I invited him to the presbytery for a beer, wondering as I said it whether it was wise even to encourage moderate drinking in one so dangerous once he had had a few. He accepted eagerly.

'I've found another woman,' he said, entering my sitting-room and perching nervously on the edge of the chair I had offered. Despite the coolness of the night he was still without a jacket and was wearing the grimy-looking shirt I had noticed before.

'Through the Internet Catholic Dating Agency?' I asked.

'Yes.'

'Do you like this one any better?'

'Perhaps. She's a nurse at the General Hospital. Quite a large woman, I suppose you'd say. I'm not really sure about it.'

He paused, and I pondered what my response should be. He was such a singularly unappealing individual that I couldn't really imagine him with any woman at all, let alone an attractive one, but it seemed best to encourage him again.

'Have you been out together yet?' I asked.

He brightened a little at this.

'Yes, we went bowling, but she broke her arm falling off a chair at the bar. I don't think we'll be meeting again for a little while because she wants time for it to heal before going out again.'

43

'I see.'

He looked troubled.

'I think she may be using it as an excuse not to see me.'

I asked whether he had made any unadvisable physical moves, or whether, aside from the broken arm, anything else had happened to make the evening less than a success.

'Well,' he said, his shoulders tensing even more than before. 'There was one thing. I made a comment about her weight. I asked her whether she had ever thought about going on a diet.'

'Do you think that was wise?'

'I'm not sure, Father Page. What do you think?'

I began to realise what I was taking on in trying to help the poor sap and told him quite firmly that if he wanted to end a relationship before it had even started, he should carry on making comments of this kind. I also told him that I thought he should abandon all hope that she might want to see him again. He seemed to accept this, and I formed an impression that my advice was very important to him. Urging him not to give up and making it clear that I had things to do, I ushered him through the door and finalised preparations for the great leap forward of the next morning.

As it turned out, things went well. The congregation was slightly bigger than normal and they made the Latin responses quite audibly. Of course, most of them were old enough to remember the old Mass and probably knew a version of the words already. Drone was there, carrying a briefcase and a rolled umbrella, but the biggest surprise was the presence of Miss Anderson. She came into the sacristy after Mass and told me that, against expectation, she had enjoyed herself.

'I really came along to see how much I would dislike it, but having the leaflet helped a lot. I particularly liked your saying the Mass the other way around.'

'Facing east?'

'Yes. Somehow it made it more spiritual. I can't explain exactly why, but it did.'

I was delighted by this favourable reaction and remembered my other incipient campaign of trying to persuade the primary school to have a look at *Dogma and Doctrine* and think twice about the dreadful, bunny rabbit-infested *Look At Me, Lord*. I asked her if she would be interested in seeing a copy of the former.

'Oh, no thanks,' she replied. 'We were warned off that when I was doing my degree. It just tells the children what to believe and doesn't give them a chance to think.'

'You should at least give it a chance. Have you ever seen a copy?'

'Well, no, actually.'

'I'll bring one round on my next visit to the school. Only, don't tell anyone - you might get into trouble.'

She smiled at this and I was glad she had not pinned me down as some reactionary ogre. After she left, Drone also put in an appearance, and by the way he was twitching his umbrella I could tell he was pleased.

'Splendid, Father, splendid,' he said in his best deadpan manner. 'I was particularly impressed by your pronunciation of the Latin and your mastery of the rubrics.'

'A bit of midnight oil went into that, I can assure you, Mr. Drone.'

'I see you decided to use the new stone altar and not the old one.'

'Yes. I thought the old one might be a bit too far away.'

'It worked perfectly well in the old days.'

I conceded the point.

He pushed off, leaving me delighted for once to feel some support for what I was doing. However, I knew that in truth this was only the calm before the storm, and that when the more vocal members of the Liturgy Group returned the real trouble would begin.

(FIVE)

The evening of the Liturgy Planning Group meeting soon came round and I have to confess that the thought of it practically ruined my day. Buller and Phillips had been strangely quiet since their return from the WAR! conference, but I was not foolish enough to be cheered by this. It was obvious that they were up to something and I had no intention of underestimating them. The evening started early with the Mice appearing to help me prepare a buffet meal for consumption after the meeting, after which the others started to trickle in. The atmosphere was sombre, Phillips and Buller arriving together and greeting me coldly when I opened the door. The former had not, unlike Buller, ever been a nun, but she remained wedded to the idea of wearing quasi-religious garb, and as usual was sporting the somewhat hieratic costume I had noticed before. Her friend, meanwhile, had evidently decided that some power-dressing was in order and had brought out the designer labels with a vengeance. The impressive, Italian-style handbag was firmly in place and I wondered what it contained this time. It was Phillips, as chair of the group, who opened the meeting.

'O.K.,' she said, 'let's not beat about the bush. Betrayal is an ugly word to have to use, but I feel it's justified. I think we all would like to know why you, James, went behind our backs and introduced a major change to the liturgy here without consultation. Further, why you confused the parishioners by delivering a reactionary talk full of erroneous and out-of-date opinions. You seem to be determined to go out of your way to blot your copybook in this parish and we, as the Liturgy Planning Group, must make sure your foolishness does no permanent harm.'

I replied in short order, telling her that although Father Hicks had set up the Liturgy Planning Group, I had no intention of treating it as any more than a consultative body. If I thought particular changes were needed in the liturgy, I would feel free to make them independently. Furthermore, I had thought through my views in detail and would recommend the group to spend some time studying the works of the Revd. Messrs. Schmidt and O'Shea, from which they would profit greatly. At this point, Buller broke in. She was undoubtedly very angry.

'Just because you've read a couple of books by two liturgical dinosaurs doesn't mean you can kill democracy in this parish,' she said. 'I propose that the group votes whether they think the Thursday, eastward facing Latin Masses should continue.'

Naturally, I was defeated by a large majority. The Mice looked incredibly guilty after the vote and I noticed one or two others looking sheepish, but for now the power of the Buller/Phillips axis was too strong to allow dissent. Made bold by this success, Phillips now outlined some further developments in the reordering project.

'As you all know,' she said, 'this has been well-prepared and thoroughly costed. The plans are ready and I am sure that no-one would now wish to delay its inception. I propose, therefore, that we hold an open meeting of the parish where the plans can be displayed and their rationale explained.'

Once again, a large majority was in favour and a date was fixed. I had not expected things to move so quickly and was unprepared what to say. However, Phillips wasn't wasting any time. She now invited Tonks to speak and he revealed that he was about to advertise a Nurdles concert in the parish hall to raise money for the reordering. Buller was then given the floor and asked me whether my speech on the liturgy had been a one-off or whether more were to be expected. I decided to come clean and revealed that Canon Taylor would be giving a talk too.

'In that case,' she said, 'I demand that my husband should also be given an opportunity to address the parish. I am sure that once a real liturgist, who actually knows what he is talking about, explains things to people, they will see how thoroughly they have been misled.'

As ever, the proposal was agreed, and I saw the cleverness of this, the aim clearly being to make the old fellow look foolish when all he had said was contradicted soon afterwards by a so-called 'real' liturgical expert. However, she wasn't finished yet.

'And now to the liturgical dance,' she said.

What fresh Hell is this? I thought.

'Even you, James,' she continued, giving me an even more withering look than normal, 'must have heard of the Sisters of Servitude.'

I said that I had.

'You will therefore be delighted to learn that they have offered to this parish their considerable expertise in the field of experimental liturgical dance. In short, they propose to assist us at next Sunday's Mass. What is more, Greg and the choir will perform the premiere of his new *People's Mass*, won't you, Greg?'

In reply, Tonks made a sort of gurgling noise that he often used as a substitute for speech when being harangued by either Phillips or Buller. I began to speculate as to what double horror awaited me. I knew that the Sisters of Servitude, a group of aged but determinedly trendy nuns, would occasionally inflict themselves on a parish and gyrate in front of the multitude, but had hoped that Cheeseminster would be exempt from their ministrations for some time to come. As for a special composition from Tonks - well, the mind boggled. Phillips now chipped in to deliver the *coup de grâce*.

'The Sisters have informed me, James, that in order to give them a suitable liturgical space in which to dance, they will need you to place the altar in the centre of the church and arrange an area around it. I am sure Desmond will help you with this after the eight o'clock Mass.'

O'Grady nodded grimly, no doubt wondering what nightmares his servers would be put through this time. I could

48

see it was game, set and match to Phillips and so decided not to voice any further objections to her plans that evening. Any counter-attack would have to wait, and as we settled down to the buffet I pondered what further miseries would have to be endured before I could send these people packing.

Despite the vote that had been taken about the Thursday Mass, I was so irritated by the way events were shaping that I decided to ignore this so-called democracy and do exactly as I had done the previous week. I had reckoned without O'Grady. When I arrived in the morning to unlock the church I found him already installed, and discovered on questioning him that Hicks had given him a set of keys before departing from the parish. A little annoyed at this, I set up the books for the Mass in the usual way before retiring to the sacristy to vest and say a few prayers. When I emerged, I found to my horror that the wooden altar had been dragged from its resting place and the Latin Missal replaced with an English one. Of O'Grady, there was no sign and I was faced with a choice of either carrying on with the materials he had given me or completely rearranging the sanctuary furniture in the presence of the congregation. I did not hesitate to do the latter.

About half-way through the Mass I noticed O'Grady suddenly emerging from behind a pillar and making a swift exit through a side door. This disturbed me so much that I completely mispronounced 'Dominus vobiscum.' At the end of the Mass I went looking for the idiotic man, but he was nowhere to be found. I could only imagine Buller and Phillips had put him up to this skulduggery, and was further staggered to receive a phone call later that morning from the diocesan Pastoral Centre, the caller being none other than my nemesis, Bernie Buller. He had already been informed of my refusal to pay any attention to the Liturgy Planning Group and proceeded to give me a lecture, laced with veiled threats, on the inadvisability of ignoring the opinions of the laity. I was informed that democracy was on the march in the Church and that if I wanted to be a successful priest in the modern world I would have to learn how to bow to the wishes of the people. The bishop's name was dropped into the conversation a couple of times, and I very much got the impression that these were more than just the personal opinions of Buller. Already, the Thursday Latin Mass was making ripples and Terry Molloy's prophecies were beginning to appear uncannily accurate.

Should I stop now, I wondered, or remain committed to a path that might eventually lead to my own destruction? As I made my way over to the school with a copy of *Dogma and Doctrine*, I pondered why I had become a priest in the first place and decided that it was not so that I could be bossed around by a bunch of ageing trendies. I would fight on, but allies were needed and maybe, just maybe, Miss Anderson would be one of them. Clutching my copy of the book I met her in the staff room, but she jumped like one of the rabbits in *Look At Me, Lord* and ushered me into what could only be described as a cupboard. This was almost more than I could cope with, for as usual she was wearing a dress with a low-cut top and such physical proximity was intoxicating. I handed her the book and she slipped it into another she was carrying.

'Will you read it?' I asked.

'Of course. But don't mention to anyone else you've given it to me. Hush, hush, all right?'

I promised and we made our exit from the cupboard. I then had a brilliant idea.

'Miss Anderson,' I said, smoothing my hair which had become ruffled. 'How would you like to join the Liturgy Planning Group?'

I could see at once that she was looking for reasons to say no and wondered how to persuade her. I could see all kinds of advantages in this plan if it was played right. The thing would be for her to approach Phillips and ask to be co-opted onto the group. Phillips would naturally mark her down as an ally, but I knew better after her comments in the wake of the first Latin Mass. I now began to flatter her for the interest she had shown in the liturgy in recent weeks and to say how much the Mice needed some help with preparing the post-meeting buffets. Since it happened that one of the Mice was her aunt, this turned out to have been exactly the right thing to say and she agreed to give it a try. I departed in high spirits and, emboldened by my success, drove out to the suburbs to try to persuade Terry Molloy to give a talk in the liturgy series as a counterweight to Bernie Buller. Although Terry was not what one might call a liturgical expert, he had obviously developed an antipathy to the Phillips crowd and was, as the canon had said, an intelligent man. I felt I could rely on him to say the right things, if only to annoy Phillips. As usual, I found him in a dreadful state, gasping at a cigarette and unshaven, the usual filthy-looking cardigan draped over his thin shoulders and the remains of a disgusting lunch littered about the kitchen.

'How's the war?' he asked.

I explained the new role I had in mind for him in the campaign and he gave me a look of dismay.

'I don't do speeches,' he said.

'But you'd be great. The parishioners love you.'

'No, they don't.'

'Of course they do. They're always asking after you, particularly the old ladies. I think they think you might die, or something. Give them a treat. Turn up in a suit and collar and let them have a bit of the old Terry Molloy, the dazzler of yesteryear. Not only that, but I'll give you a bottle of whisky into the bargain.'

'Old Fetterfiddich?'

'If you like.'

I could see he was wavering.

'Done,' he said at last. 'I suppose I ought to help you out. Your Campaign for Better Liturgy is already making waves in the diocese. Only this morning I had a ring from Dermot Byrne, asking if you'd gone mad.'

'Dermot Byrne, the Beast of Chedderford?'

'The very man.'

Byrne and Molloy had been in the seminary together and, of the two of them, the former had been an even bigger thorn in the backside for the bishop than the latter. At diocesan retreats they were usually the two who spent most time propping up the bar.

'Does he think I'm wrong to do what I'm doing?' I asked.

'On the contrary, he's right behind you, but he still thinks you're mad. Even he hasn't done a Latin Mass, though I wouldn't put it past him, if only to annoy the clowns at HQ. You and he should get in touch. He's a bit bored at the moment and looking for some trouble. He's also a great pal of Dr. Petroc Tomkinson, who could be very useful to you indeed.'

I asked him to elucidate.

'Tomkinson's that chap who got pushed into taking early retirement from the seminary for being a fuddy-duddy. Canon Taylor's all very well, but you'll need bigger guns than him to see off Bernie Buller. Old Petroc might just be your man. I'll give Dermot a ring and see what he can do.'

I was beginning to feel that Terry, despite his natural apathy, was starting to take a genuine interest in my crusade, and left him to his afternoon considerably cheered by the axis that was forming in my favour. I was evidently not entirely without allies in the fight, and although the ageing trendies held the field for the moment I was not without hope now that a rout might be averted. In this mood I returned to the presbytery and braced myself for what next Sunday would bring.

SIX

Though the memory makes me shudder I think I should, for the record, explain what happened at the *People's Mass*.

The choir were in early, rehearsing and rehearsing the garbage that Tonks had lovingly composed during his summer break at Torquay. He had written an opening hymn, a *Gloria*, a *Creed*, a special *Agnus Dei* and a kind of recessional dirge to which he seemed particularly attached. Two saxophone players had been brought in to add to the racket, as well as a couple of flautists and a few additional guitarists. Several members of the Nurdles had agreed to play and the choir was augmented by some hairy types who were normally to be found at the bar of the Frog and Ferret. All in all, this took up quite a lot of space, but they had installed themselves in the area normally containing the sanctuary to allow the Sisters of Servitude free rein on what could only now be described as the dance floor. To add to the confusion, O'Grady had clearly called up every altar server on his list, and before the Mass the sacristy was awash with a horde of children, ranging from tiny tots who could hardly walk to strapping teenagers in training shoes and Moroccan garb, all making a racket of epic proportions. The procession was to be preceded by the nuns, five geriatric biddies wearing outsize cloaks and looking as if the exertion might prove their undoing. Tonks had explained in the course of a lengthy telephone conversation the night before that the opening hymn was called *All People Clap Your Hands and Praise the God of Dance*, so I was under no illusions what we were in for.

Things unfolded at a rapid pace. After the bell was rung for the start of Mass the nuns began clapping rhythmically and swaying from side to side. As yet they didn't move forward and Tonks' immense orchestra was hushed. Then, in a scene straight out of a pensioners' version of *Sister*

53

Act, the nuns boldly set forth, repetitively singing the words of the title and letting out the occasional yelp. At this point Tonks' choir joined in, and before long a blare of saxophones was accompanying them. I soon realised that Tonks' skills as a lyricist did not run to providing any more words than those in the title, and that what we were going to get was endless repetition of the same. Meanwhile the servers, egged on by O'Grady, also clapped in an embarrassed sort of way, the embarrassment rising with the age of the server, while I kept my head down and tried to think of Palestrina.

It was soon clear that the Sisters of Servitude had no intention of simply heading straight from the sacristy to our ultimate destination, the altar rigged up where the aisle had once been, but were determined to weave this way and that around the congregation, nodding their heads furiously to the rhythm while clapping as if their lives depended on it. By the time we actually reached the altar I for one was exhausted, and the sisters themselves looked far from fresh. However, Tonks and his crew were still going strong, and we all stood there like lemons while the choir continued to exhort people to praise the God of dance by clapping their hands. The congregation, however, apart from some deranged old codgers in the front row, had clearly had enough, and the bearded one was eventually forced to take the hint, dropping his arms reluctantly and telling the orchestra to give it a rest. It was only now that I noticed he was wearing some sort of rainbow-coloured cape to mark the occasion, completing the *Lord of the Rings*-meets-Harry Potter feel that the Mass was taking on.

Repressing the urge to turn everything on its head by saying 'Dominus vobiscum', I did the little bit assigned to me before the *Gloria*, after which the nuns set off again, dancing their way in ecstatic fashion around the makeshift sanctuary as the word 'Gloria' was repeated about a hundred and fifty times. Fed up, I decided to sit down, wondering why I had not brought with me that morning's copy of the *Sunday Telegraph* to while away the time. The offertory procession gave the wheezing sisters yet further scope for their terpsichorean talents, and I noticed another gross departure from normal practice during the Eucharistic Prayer when the entire congregation, bar a few diehards, were told by Tonks to stand rather than kneel. This, as I saw later, had been ordered in the leaflet produced by Phillips to accompany the Mass, a production that bore all the hallmarks of the Bernie Buller school of liturgy. It was one of the staple orthodoxies of his kind that kneeling was a servile posture that should be driven ruthlessly from the modern Mass, and I was annoyed that I had not been able to put a stop its abandonment here.

Finally, about two and a half hours later, we reached the end and processed out to some dreadful stuff about 'Go, go, go, let's follow the Lord, the Lord is love, to be adored', and as soon as I managed to quit the church and gain the safe harbour of the presbytery I reached frantically for the whisky bottle. If the Mass just endured were ever repeated, I knew for a fact that I would be asking for a transfer to a Carthusian monastery, and was therefore far from pleased when my afternoon nap was interrupted by a knock at the door and I found myself face to face with Mark Spooner.

For once, he was not alone. Standing just behind him and looking immensely sheepish was what at first sight appeared to be a fifteen year old girl. On closer inspection she turned out to be a fraction older, but she was so small and slight and with such girlish features that my initial misapprehension was wholly understandable. Spooner was, as usual, dressed in his trademark unironed shirt and scruffy trousers, while the girl wore a summer dress marked with a flowery pattern, white socks and training shoes. Her hair was arranged into two pigtails and she wore enormous bottle spectacles, as if to all intents and purposes blind. I repressed the uncharitable thought that blindness might be a positive asset in going out with Spooner and asked them if they'd like to come in and have a cup of tea. Spooner declined.

'No thank you, Father,' he said. 'We only came to say hello. Janet wanted to meet you after I had told her so much about you. We're off to a science fair at the university.'

'I'm a student too,' said the girl, in a rather breathless, squeaky voice.

'Oh? So you didn't meet via the dating agency, then?'

As soon as I'd said it I knew I'd made a mistake, for Spooner went bright red and the girl looked at him quizzically.

'Er, no, Father,' he said hastily. 'No. We met at the bar in the Engineering Faculty.'

A silence ensued, Spooner rubbing one leg against the back of the other while the girl stared at the ground, evidently embarrassed. I wondered what I could say to rescue the situation, but no words came. Fortunately, we were saved by the arrival of one of my regular callers, a tramp named O'Flaherty, and Spooner and the girl took their leave, though not before the tramp had had a chance to give them a good looking over, perhaps reflecting that he wasn't the worst dressed man in Cheeseminster after all.

By the time I'd finished with O'Flaherty and completed my interrupted nap, I was ready to reconsider the parish situation. The Mass had made me so angry that I felt ready now to carry the battle to the enemy and go several steps further in my campaign against the Cheeseminster modernists. What had I actually achieved so far? Very little in reality, and although the reaction had been hysterical, that was simply because my opponents were so unused to having anything less than enthusiastic approval for their plans. What I needed was to open several more fronts at once and to follow the internal logic of what I had already started. If I really believed what Schmidt and O'Shea were saying, why didn't I move things along a little and apply a few more of their ideas. After all, when all was said and done I was still the parish priest, and if I wanted to change things in the interest of what I believed to be right, then so be it. There was nothing to fear, really, but my own timidity. The reordering was to be opposed at every turn, of course, but I could force myself to be a little more pro-active than that. I started to make a list of all the things that needed to be done. Eventually, I settled on ten critical points:

1) Wind up the Liturgy Planning Group
2) No reordering
3) Tonks out
4) O'Grady out
5) Latin in all the Masses
6) Sling out the third altar
7) All Masses said facing east
8) Bring back the altar rails and kneeling at communion
9) Reintroduce communion on the tongue
10) Get rid of the extraordinary ministers

As a wish list, this was pretty thoroughgoing stuff, but there was no harm in making a start. I therefore decided to kick things off by shoving the wooden/cardboard altar into the back of the car and taking it to the municipal dump. Good riddance to that, then. If O'Grady was so attached to it, he could pick it up and use it at home. I felt much better after this, and driving back began to think how I could address the other issues on my list.

The question of the extraordinary ministers was a particularly difficult one. These were the large numbers of men and women commissioned by my modernist predecessor to help him administer communion, a practice that had only originally been brought in, as the name suggests, for use in extraordinary circumstances. However, as usual, abuses had soon crept in and now the sanctuary was packed with them at every Sunday Mass, leaving me, the poor priest, with very little to do. Since I was the one ordained to administer communion, it seemed quite wrong that my functions had been usurped in this way, but to sack the ministers would cause all kinds of ructions and would need careful handling. The people who had been duped into taking on the task were no doubt unaware that they were not supposed to be a regular feature of every Mass, and to explain that they had been misled would be difficult.

As for the altar rails, this was also a tricky area as the originals had no doubt been destroyed years ago. However, I had been convinced by my reading that the practice of communion in the hand was another modern heresy and that far greater reverence would be achieved if we reverted to the traditional practice of kneeling to receive the host on the tongue. For that, you needed an altar rail for people to kneel against, and I began to wrack my brains to see if there were any way of getting hold of one. It then struck me that a reordering process similar to that destined for Cheeseminster had just begun over at Stapleford and that the church there, through some minor miracle, had not until now had its altar rails removed. The church, I recollected, had been built at roughly the same period as mine and the sanctuary was of an approximately similar size.

On reaching home, I rang the parish priest and asked what he had done with the rails, discovering that they had been dumped in his garage prior to being carted away for destruction. When I asked if I could have them, he professed astonishment and demanded to know what on earth I could possibly want with some old pieces of wood. Rather than telling him the truth, which he probably wouldn't have believed anyway, I said that I enjoyed collecting redundant ecclesiastical artefacts and would be grateful if he could humour a harmless eccentric by allowing me to add them to my collection. He said I could take them whenever I liked.

I now rang up Miss Anderson, apologising for disturbing her well-earned Sunday rest and asked if the school had any kind of minibus or van that could be used for transporting large, wooden objects. The answer to this was no, but it turned out that her boyfriend was a builder and had just the thing. Despite my protests that the matter was not urgent enough for her to do anything about it straight away, she rang him and within half an hour the two of them were pulling up outside the presbytery in the desired vehicle. The boyfriend, named Ray, turned out to be an exceptionally affable fellow and a parishioner of Terry Molloy's. He said he often did odd jobs for Terry and would be glad to run out to Stapleford for me. I then squeezed into the front of the van next to Julia, as she now insisted on my calling her, and we headed out into the country. En route, I asked if she'd had a chance to look at *Dogma and Doctrine*.

'Yes,' she said, 'I have.'

'Your verdict?'

'Well, I think we most have been brainwashed at college. It's actually very good. I mean, the title's rather off-putting and there are a lot less pictures, but I think the children would like it. Actually, I learned a lot more about Catholicism by reading it than I knew before. To be honest with you, Father, they were using *Look At Me, Lord* when I was at school, so I don't know as much about religion as you might think. I suppose I was a bit embarrassed about that, so the vagueness of *Look At Me, Lord* gave me something to hide behind.'

'Would you mind talking to the Head of RE about it?' I asked, immensely cheered by her reaction.

'I am the Head of RE,' she replied.

'Fantastic.'

'It's not as simple as that.'

I knew what she meant, aware that this was not simply a matter of her personal choice, so said I would talk to her boss about it and possibly to the diocesan Education Office as well. I needed to know how vigorous the prohibition was on other textbooks before we took the matter any further.

On arrival at Stapleford, the parish priest, a man whom I knew only vaguely, showed me to the garage and let us get on with the business of removing the rails. The moment I saw them I knew they would be perfect, and reflected that my daily Rosary was swiftly producing even more dividends than I'd imagined. The rails were not too heavy and came in four pieces, meaning that the three of us could get them into the van without undue difficulty. They were also remarkably clean, so putting them in position on our return to Cheeseminster did not involve much work. Julia said that the original rails in the church, which she remembered from her childhood, had not been very different, and I thanked her and Ray for their help before returning to the presbytery a happy man.

It was now late and the evening too far gone to address any more of my ten 'theses', so I decided to call it a day. Before going to bed I wondered whether, in imitation of Luther, I should nail them to the door of the church, but decided that the precedent was not, perhaps, altogether a happy one. The following morning I put out the Latin/English Mass leaflets in the porch and announced that henceforth all weekday Masses would be like the Thursday one. I also drew the congregation's attention to the altar rails and said that I would prefer it if they knelt for communion and received the host on the tongue. I told them that Canon Taylor would shortly be giving a talk on that very subject and if they wanted to know why this was my preferred practice, they would find out then. The old buffer and I had agreed a few days before that this would be his topic, the area being one in which he was a genuine specialist, having been a pupil of the great Australian liturgist Milo O'Strange. Most of the tiny congregation acceded to my wishes, but one rather feisty old bird stormed into the sacristy after Mass and said that she had had just about enough of my meddling and wanted to know when it would stop. I was subjected to a rant about the evils of the Bad Old Days and how a young whippersnapper like myself could not possibly know how awful things had been before the Council. She declared her intention to complain to all and sundry and notably to Miranda Phillips.

She was swiftly followed by O'Grady, who had lurked at the back throughout the Mass and now demanded to know what I had done with his beloved cardboard altar.

'It's in the bin,' I said, 'Or rather, the municipal dump. Go and get it if you like, but don't bring it back here.'

For a moment he was speechless, but his expression betrayed the rage that was building inside him. I could see he was searching for a suitably stinging reply.

'Then you have my resignation,' he said at last, before turning heel in a rather dramatic manner and tripping over a thurible on his way out.

I couldn't believe my luck. Another of my aims rapidly achieved without me having to do a thing. Next in was Hubert Drone, looking more chuffed than ever, though as usual dressed for a funeral. He was clutching at his briefcase rather more tightly than usual and the umbrella was in full twirl.

'Father,' he said, 'I take my hat off to you. What you have done demanded great courage. You are a credit to your cloth. I wonder if I might now be so bold as to make you a proposition.'

He outlined his idea. Canon Taylor had, apparently, told him that week that the monthly old rite Masses at Muckford would have to cease as he no longer felt up to continuing them. The local hospital had confirmed that a major operation, for which he had been waiting for some time, could now be performed and he would be incapacitated for some time. In short, demanded Drone, would I, Father Page, be prepared to say the monthly Mass for the CRS, here at St. Aelred's, Cheeseminster. I asked him at what time these Masses occurred.

'Three o'clock,' he replied.

'I see.'

This was not good. I was greatly wedded to the concept of my Sunday siesta and did not relish it being taken away. Furthermore, I would have to learn how to say the old rite, which to my knowledge was a great deal more complicated than the new. I told Drone I would think about it and he toddled off, more than happy, it seemed, with my reply.

I moved across to the presbytery for my toast and marmalade and reflected on the work of the last twenty-four hours. Pondering the likely response from Buller and company to what I had done, my courage failed me a little, but there was no going back now and so I drove over to Muckford and discussed with Canon Taylor the contents of his talk. Before leaving, I asked him if he could let me have a copy of the old rite of Mass so that I could see if I felt up to saying it. I returned to find Lavender Buller ringing the presbytery doorbell.

'Ah, there you are, James,' she said. 'I thought you were hiding from me. Now what's all this I hear about altar rails and Latin Masses?'

Without inviting her in, I explained what I had done. I had never in my life heard anyone snort before, but she snorted now.

'We'll see about this,' she said, evidently extremely angry. 'What you probably don't know is that WAR! are very influential at Bishop's House and that furthermore my husband has a great deal of clout. Trying to turn the clock back to the dark ages won't do you any good. Why would a man of your age want to do this, anyway? Are you looking for trouble? It wouldn't surprise me if you started saying old rite Masses next.'

I told her I was thinking about doing just that.

'Well, that's just about all I'm going to take from you today,' she sniffed. 'Tell me now: do you or do you not intend continuing with these ludicrous Latin Masses during the week?'

'Yes, I do.'

'With your back to the people?'

'If you mean facing east and leading the congregation in prayer, then, yes.'

She gave me a look of contempt, mingled with a fair degree of loathing.

'Thank you,' she said. 'That's all I needed to know. You do realise this is only the beginning, I suppose? If you intend to carry on like this, I think you may as well start packing your bags now. You can't fight us, you know, with your pathetic, reactionary ideas. As someone once said, we are the masters now.'

With a coolness I could only admire she got into her car without so much as a backward glance and drove off, leaving me rather winded by the encounter. However, before I could really think through what she had said another vehicle pulled up and Tonks emerged from a small, white van, accompanied by one of the hairy men who had helped him out on Sunday with the choir.

'Hello, there, Jim,' he said, cheerfully. 'I need the keys to the parish hall. We're setting up for tonight's Nurdles gig.'

'Nurdles gig?' I said, baffled by what appeared to be a foreign language.

'Yes, you remember. The charity gig for the reordering.'

'Oh, that.'

Some light began to dawn. Tonks now decided it was time I was introduced to his friend.

'Have you met Jethro?' he asked.

I shook hands with him and he asked my opinion of the music at the Mass.

'I have to be honest,' I said. 'I don't think that sort of thing is suitable for the liturgy. I think, Greg, we need to discuss it at the planning group.'

These remarks were greeted by twin, malevolent stares and I could see I had gone too far once again. Eventually, Tonks spoke.

'It took me three weeks to prepare for that Mass, Father,' he said. 'Not forgetting the rehearsals and all the rest of it. It won't be long before we record it on CD. I think your remarks only go to reveal your ignorance. I suppose you'd prefer something in Latin?'

'Well, yes, actually.'

I received my second snort of the day, and the two of them pushed off towards the hall. As I went in search of the keys, I wondered how much contempt I could cope with all at once.

Soon, a dreadful noise began to emanate from the building, evidently the sound of the Nurdles rehearsing. I knew I had no option but to attend the concert, despite the fact that all my new-found enemies would be there. I had even made the mistake of offering to help behind the bar. Soon a gaggle of people wearing corduroy trousers and sandals began to filter past the presbytery into the hall and I entered to find things in full swing. Cider was being drunk in quantity and beards were much in evidence. Before long Tonks appeared on the stage and said that their first number would be an old favourite called *The Nurdling Gurdler*.

Now, I am no expert on West Country dialect, despite coming from the area myself, but the lyrics of this song would surely have been incomprehensible to all but the most diehard cornwangler, or whatever the word is. It was explained to me later that gurdling was a process connected with the churning of cheese and that nurdling was a dialect term for singing. This was all news to me, but a red-faced, bottle-nosed man to my right assured me that the song was a great favourite and was constantly being played on local radio. Since about the only channels I ever listen to are Radios Three and Four, I was, I reflected, unlikely to have heard of it. The band then launched into *I'm a Nuzzler*, which sounded rather rude, and *The Ballad of Old Neddy*, an agricultural song which, the bottle-nosed one assured me, was of ancient provenance. Certainly, quite a few people seemed keen to sing along, including O'Grady, who was dressed in a check shirt and cravat. He had pointedly ignored me on coming in, but was now knocking back the cider with gusto and smoking a clay pipe. Since he was obviously of Irish parentage, this struck me as just a trifle inauthentic.

All went well until the interval, when pork pies were consumed, along with large quantities of a blue-veined local cheese that everyone in these parts seems to swear by. Smoke from the assembled pipes, cigars and cigarettes rose in a dense cloud, and I began to feel nauseous. I went outside for a breath of fresh air and returned to find the concert in full swing again, with Tonks hamming it up on stage in no uncertain manner while clutching what could only be described as a flagon of ale. The song was evidently of the farmyard variety, with animal noises greatly in evidence, Tonks being required to imitate the animals as they came round in the chorus.

It was when he was well into his rather strutting imitation of a turkey for the third time that disaster struck. In the course of all the prancing about, much beer had been spilt, and as Tonks clucked and flapped away he suddenly slipped and went careering off the stage into the front two rows of the audience. Everyone clapped and cheered, thinking this was part of the act, and it was only when the clucking stopped and Tonks failed to emerge that the accidental nature of his fall became obvious.

The band stopped the song, and eventually an ambulance arrived to haul the singer off. It was obvious that Tonks would not be fit to appear at Mass next Sunday: the *People's Mass* had been his swansong.

SEVEN

I had forgotten that O'Grady still had his keys. The next day I opened the church to find that the altar rails were no more and that the cardboard monstrosity was back in place. O'Grady had actually gone all the way to the dump to retrieve it. There was nothing for it this time, so I took it into the back yard, smashed it to pieces with an axe and set fire to what was left.

'Let him rescue that,' I thought as I headed back to the church. After Mass I telephoned the police to inform them of the theft of the altar rails and explained that an interview with O'Grady might not be such a bad idea. In the end, this was not needed. It turned out that accompanied by his son Jim, one of the more obstreperous altar servers, he had bundled the rails into the back of his 4x4 – no mean feat given their size – and headed for the dump. Divine wrath was obviously on his tail, however, for O'Grady had swiftly managed to reverse into a dustcart and done considerable damage to the car, as well as blocking the A354 for most of the morning. When the rails finally arrived back in the church, courtesy once again of Julia's boyfriend, they were a little tarnished but otherwise none the worse for their adventure. I asked Ray if he could fix them to the floor.

'No problem, Father,' he said, 'You've obviously got a maniac on your hands.'

The next morning, things were, if anything, worse. About twenty ladies of a certain age greeted me as I tried to enter the church, holding a large banner emblazoned with the words 'WE ARE RIGHT!' and chanting 'War!' at the top of their voices. A local newspaper reporter was taking notes. About halfway through the Mass the women marched down the aisle and took up the chanting again before depositing some leaflets and pushing off. The reporter was waiting for me in the sacristy afterwards, but I was in no mood to talk.

66

Instead, I muttered a swift 'no comment' and then headed for breakfast. The article duly appeared the following day, laced with comments from Buller and O'Grady and giving a decidedly one-sided story of recent events. I was branded an obscurantist who wanted to drag the parish back into the Middle Ages and who had treated highhandedly a democratically elected parish committee. I had also, apparently, seen off my chief altar server and insulted the choir. There was even an interview with Tonks from his hospital bed, quoting what I had said about the *People's Mass*. It was a complete rout.

Needless to say, the phone rang all morning, among the calls being an urgent request from the bishop's secretary to come down to Bishop's House at Gorgehampton and talk with him at once. Fortunately, his Lordship was not in residence, but he had been apprised of the situation and I was strongly urged by the secretary to make my peace with Buller and friends to avoid any further scandal for the diocese. I replied that it was Buller who had created the scandal by calling the press. I was then advised that it was not very sensible to start bringing in Latin Masses and saying Mass with my back to the people, and that the bishop took a very dim view of such a promising young priest suddenly going off the rails like this. Why, if things got any worse I might be obliged to take a 'sabbatical', code, I knew, for losing the parish and undergoing a year's brainwashing at a pastoral centre in another diocese. When I began to quote Schmidt and O'Shea, I was told that their writ did not run in this part of Christendom and that a more pastoral approach to liturgy was the norm. I decided to shut up and leave before I lost my temper.

Later, I drove over to Muckford to pick the canon up before his talk and discussed with him what had happened.

'The modern Church needs martyrs,' he said, laconically. 'Round here, looks like you're going to be the first.'

After the rumpus of the last few days, I was expecting a great deal of interest in the talk and was not disappointed. The hall, not a particularly large venue, was full to bursting, and I noticed that this time the modernists were out in force. The two Bullers were both there, as were Phillips and O'Grady, but batting for the traditionalists were Terry Molloy and Drone, so I did not feel entirely isolated. Molloy had even taken my hint about smartening himself up a bit, for he had shaved and gone so far as to wear a jacket and clerical collar. Many of the parishioners were clearly delighted to see him, and I heard some promises being made to take some cakes over to his parish to ensure he didn't die.

The canon, for all his ninety-three years, was on fine form, showing comprehensively, at least to me, that the practice of communion on the tongue should be the norm for Catholics everywhere. This question must seem rather esoteric to non-Catholics, but on it rides the whole matter of reverence to the Sacred Species. Canon Taylor was able to show that the reason why the Church had adopted this manner of giving communion was in response to a developed understanding of the sacredness of the host, and that the reintroduction of communion in the hand had led to a great number of abuses. He reminded his audience that the current Pope had shown most strongly his dislike of this change, and that when polled in the nineteen-sixties, most of the world's bishops had come out against it. Furthermore, Mother Theresa had condemned it as the greatest abuse going on in the Church today. Quoting from a number of scholars and bishops who had written on the subject, the canon showed clearly that communion in the hand was an example of what Pope Pius XII had called false archeologism, a desire to return to the practices of the very early Church despite the fact that these same practices had been abandoned to prevent abuses.

I wondered how the WAR! faction in the audience was going to handle all this. I was sure Bernie Buller could quote any amount of gobbledegook by means of counter-argument, all designed to show that abuses were much rarer than the canon made out and that a return to the pure sources of early church practice was always to be preferred to paying any attention to tradition. However, he said not a word throughout the discussion that followed, merely staring moodily at whoever happened to be speaking as if bored by the ramblings of such appalling low-brows. It soon became clear that he had decided to reserve his firepower for his own talk a few weeks later. Instead, he let his wife do most of the talking, with Phillips chipping in occasionally, while the majority of the audience kept their mouths firmly shut.

As chairman of the discussion, I felt my opponents had better have their say, especially as I knew that the canon was a respected figure in the diocese and that criticisms of his talk might easily backfire on the radicals. It was my secret conviction, backed up by later events, that clergy-bating was the hobby of a few over-educated middle class troublemakers, and that the majority of Catholics in the diocese had merely gone along with the changes introduced because they felt they had to. Now that they had been given chapter and verse as to why one of the biggest upheavals of the lot had not only been unnecessary but was positively bad, they might start questioning all the other horrors that had been brought in with it. For quite a while, Buller and Phillips hogged the debate and seemed determined to patronise the canon, speaking much longer than was necessary to make their rather tedious points. Happily, most of those who spoke afterwards expressed their amazement that they had never heard the other side of the argument before, and seemed indignant to have been taken in so comprehensively by the modernists. When Terry Molloy made a brief speech in support of the canon, the mood moved even further in the right direction, and at the end everyone filed out in subdued fashion, the enemy temporarily in retreat.

The following day I had a conversation with a reporter from the *Cheeseminster Echo*, the paper which had so erroneously reported what was going on in the parish, and was rewarded with a full scale interview for their *Fromage Faith* column, as well as a large picture of myself smiling benignly outside the church. After this, the phone started ringing again, most of the hostility this time coming from my fellow priests in the diocese. I learned among other things that I was a publicity-seeking young fogy who should never have been ordained for a forward-thinking diocese like Gorgehampton and who should think long and hard about all the damage he was causing. Most of the positive calls came from people revealing themselves as members of the Campaign for Real Catholicism and asking me whether it was true that I was going to say the old rite Mass for them.

As for the weekday Masses, they quietened down and began to seem quite normal to me, my fluency with the Latin continuing to improve along with the congregation's agility with the responses. Julia Anderson still appeared on quite a regular basis, along with Hubert Drone and a number of people whom he introduced to me as members of the CRC. There was even one rather perverse old woman who turned out to be a member of both the CRC and WAR!, and I asked her how on earth she managed to square that particular circle.

'Well, it's like this, James,' she said. 'I am, as they say, a bit of a radical, but I actually like the beauty of the old Mass, especially when it's sung and accompanied by Gregorian Chant. If you ever manage to get rid of that cowboy Tonks, I'd be quite happy to run a choir for you. I was kicked out in the seventies when Father Whoever It Was back then decided that guitars were the thing of the future.'

Drone assured me that she was the genuine article and I told her I would remember her offer. The mention of Tonks made me feel guilty that I had not yet visited him in hospital, so I bought a bag of grapes and drove over to Gorgehampton General. He didn't exactly seem pleased to see me.

'Oh, it's you,' he said.

His beard had grown more bushy since his hospitalisation and he now looked more pixie-like than ever. He stared at me over the sheets, looking rather sorry for himself, and I asked him how serious his injury was.

'I'll be out for weeks,' he replied. 'We've had to cancel several Nurdles gigs and I've told the choir they can take a holiday. You'll just have to manage without them.'

'I'm sorry,' I said.

'No, you're not. Judging by your comments the other day, I bet you're delighted.'

I didn't know what to say. After all, I *was* delighted, but didn't particularly want to rub it in. In the end, I said nothing.

'I see you've been in the papers again,' he remarked, eyeing up the grapes in a rather hungry manner. 'I must say, you've got some funny ideas. I mean, how can you have a folk choir with a Latin Mass? I bet Lavender Buller isn't too happy. I suppose she's going to try and get rid of you.'

'Perhaps.'

'Quite frankly, it would probably be better if she did. I don't mean to sound rude, Father, but you're not the kind of priest we want in the parish.'

I tried not to appear upset.

'Not everybody thinks that.'

'Maybe not. All the same, I think, on reflection, it might be better if the choir didn't perform at all until this mess has been sorted out. In any case, we'll have to go on strike as a mark of solidarity with Desmond and his altar servers. I've been thinking about this a lot and now I've made up my mind, so there's no point trying to talk me out of it.'

I offered him the grapes and he snatched at them greedily. It was, I hoped, the end of an era for Cheeseminster.

71

(EIGHT)

The next Sunday, the eleven o'clock Mass was of necessity a strange, silent affair. In fact, it was very much like the eight o'clock, except for the ubiquitous extraordinary ministers. I decided to tackle this business head on after the Mass and took on one side the rather polite man who was in charge of organising them.

'So,' I said, 'heady times for the parish, eh? No choir and only one altar server.'

'Yes, Father,' he replied, cheerfully. 'Is he some kind of blackleg?'

'I don't think he's in the union at all.'

In fact, it was Mark Spooner, whom I had grabbed just before Mass. He was in rather an excitable state and asked if he could see me afterwards, an appointment to which I agreed after persuading him to take on the serving.

'Well, Mr. Peterson,' I said, 'what does Mrs Buller think about it all?'

A look of pain passed across his face.

'Between you and me, Father,' he replied, seeming rather embarrassed, 'she wants to pull the extraordinary ministers out as well, but I persuaded her to let us finish the rota. I didn't want to let you down.'

I applauded the man's loyalty.

'That's very generous of you,' I said, 'but there's really no need. I have no wish to antagonise Mrs. Buller further. I think it might be better for all concerned if you took a holiday, at least until this strike business has blown over.'

He seemed relieved by my decision.

'Whatever you say. To be honest with you, Father, it will get her off my back. Miss Phillips and her keep ringing me up at all hours of the day and night about this and I've just about had enough.'

I couldn't help feeling that the enemy were playing right into my hands. I suppose they were counting on a finish to the death and my imminent removal, after which the status quo would return, but at least for the present things were going my way. Without the ministers, I had the perfect excuse to eliminate communion under both kinds and revert simply to administering the host. In Catholic teaching, this is just as good as giving out both and further obviates the need for a lot of lay assistance. Another article of faith with the modernists, however, was that the people would feel deprived unless they had the chance to drink from the chalice, but as usual it was a history of a push from above rather than a clamour from below. Canon Taylor had covered this in his talk and prepared the way for me to make a change back to more traditional practices. I had taken care to make copies of the talk available after both Masses, putting loyal members of the congregation in charge of the distribution so that the WAR! crowd didn't try to swipe them. The new dispensation could now start next week, and not a day too soon.

As Spooner cleared up after Mass I was approached by Drone, who asked me if I had decided yet about whether I would say the old rite Masses. By now I'd had a chance to study the missals lent me by Canon Taylor, and had begun to understand just how different this Mass was. The changes introduced in 1970 had indeed been profound, effectively, in my view, creating quite a different species of Mass from what had existed before. By now, of course, I had become accustomed to saying the new Mass in Latin, but taking on the old rite demanded more than simply a grasp of the ancient language. The structure of the two Masses was loosely the same, but many prayers had been altered or cut at the time of the change and a far greater number of variables introduced. There was a way of selecting these variables that brought the new rite closer to the old, and it was these I had been using during the week. Yet the instructions or rubrics that went with the older Mass had been much more precise and greater in number, meaning that if I were to say this Mass once a month

I would have to keep my wits about me. However, I allowed Drone to understand that I would be prepared to do it on an experimental basis, the condition being that I was able to adapt myself comfortably and that the current pressures in the parish did not become too overwhelming. He seemed satisfied with this, a twirl or two of the umbrella being enough to tell me of his pleasure that the Masses would continue. I reflected as I went in search of Spooner that at least it would annoy the modernists and give them, if they wanted it, further evidence that I was off my rocker.

I found Spooner outside the presbytery, biting rather furtively at his nails and smoking the inevitable cigarette. He looked even worse than normal. His rather lanky hair appeared unwashed and unkempt and his body odour, as we entered the house, struck me as almost as rank as O'Grady's. Furthermore, there were some rather foul stains down the front of his shirt. As soon as he sat down he began his litany of misery.

'I don't know what to do, Father,' he moaned, beginning to rub his hands up and down his thighs and biting his lower lip. 'Nothing ever goes right. I am a complete failure with the opposite sex.'

He seemed on the edge of tears and I braced myself for another tense session.

'What happened to that girl you were with last week?' I asked, surprised that it had ended so quickly.

'She's gone. When she heard I'd been using internet dating the heat seemed to go out of our relationship.'

I now felt rather guilty.

'I'm sorry,' I said. 'That's rather my fault, isn't it? I gave the game away about the dating when you were last here.'

'Oh, it wasn't just that. There was also a rather unfortunate incident with my car. You see, it's a bit of an old banger and I don't belong to the AA. We had driven out to the Blacksmith's Arms over at Chewton Magna, and when we were on the way back we broke down. I told her that we'd better go and look for a bus, but then it began to rain and she

74

wasn't wearing a coat. We tried to cross a field and a herd of cows went after us. She slipped in the mud and when she got up she started punching me. Then she ran off and I haven't seen her since. I don't know what I'm going to do.'

'Do you like her?' I asked, wondering whether it was worth asking any more.

'Not really. She was very boring and kept talking about bell-ringing.'

'Why?'

'It's her hobby. She made it sound very dull, but I couldn't get her to shut up about it. In fact, now I think about it, I was rather glad she fell in the mud. When I got home I laughed.'

He seemed about to laugh now, but more from hysteria than joy. I made him a cup of coffee.

'Now look, Mark,' I said, trying as usual to think of ways of encouraging him. 'Relationships are not always easy. Just because I'm a priest doesn't mean to say that I don't know that. Why, I had two very serious relationships before I decided to enter the seminary. Both went wrong in their own way.'

This did not appear to cheer him.

'Why?' he asked.

'Because in the end we weren't suited. Actually, that's not strictly true,' I reflected, casting my mind back to those rather trying times in my twenties. 'The first one ended because she wasn't really interested, and the second one because she moved to Canada. Nevertheless, I do want to encourage you to keep on with what you've started. Have you looked at the internet recently?'

He began to be a little more positive.

'Yes, there's someone there who looks quite good. But she lives in Bristol.'

'Well, that's not the end of the world, is it? Why not see if she's interested?'

'All right, I'll give it a go. Thanks very much for your help, Father.'

75

He now seemed to have recovered his equilibrium a little, and recovered it even further when we emerged from the presbytery to find Julia Anderson walking up the path. Spooner's eyes practically popped out of his head. I asked Julia if she wanted to talk to me, but it turned out that she was car-less and had missed her bus after Mass.

'Where's Ray?' I asked.

'That's why I haven't got my car. He's borrowing it for a job.'

I could almost hear Spooner's brain whirring around beside me.

'It's all right,' he said abruptly. 'I can give you a lift. I'm going that way.'

'But I haven't said where I'm going yet,' said Julia, evidently rather surprised at being addressed by him.

'Well, where is it?'

She named a suburb of Cheeseminster.

'Right on my route,' he said, more than a touch over-eagerly.

I was puzzled.

'I thought you said your car had broken down.'

'Well it's fixed now, isn't it,' he replied, looking more manic than ever. 'That's it, over there.'

He pointed to a rust bucket that seemed to have at least two of its wheels in the grave. I could see that Julia was wondering whether to accept this rather dubious offer from someone who must have looked to her like an unusually scrawny serial-killer, but in the end desperation clearly won the day. I waved them off and then returned to the presbytery to eat a late lunch.

That evening, Spooner rang me in a very excitable state.

'She's amazing, isn't she, Father?'

'Who?'

'That girl you introduced me to today. What's her name? I didn't catch it in all the excitement.'

'Julia Anderson. But you're wasting your time, Mark. She's already got a boyfriend and he's much bigger than you. My advice is, get back to your computer. Julia is not an option.'

There was a long pause and I thought he might have disappeared to slash his wrists. However, in the end he rang off without further incident and I was able to settle down to drawing up the next stage of my reforms. Looking at the list over a cup of coffee the following morning, I saw that I had in fact already achieved many of my objectives. There seemed now to be three main things to do.

First of all, Latin had to be introduced at the Sunday eight o'clock Mass. The introduction of Latin on a Sunday was a much greater step than bringing it in on a weekday, but I now felt that the moment was right. My plan for the eleven o'clock was rather different and involved approaching the CRC woman who had spoken to me during the week with regard to Gregorian chant. If she were still willing, I would ask her to form a choir to sing certain parts of the Mass – the *Gloria* and *Creed* and suchlike - in Latin, but would keep the rest of it in English. This, for the moment, seemed a sensible compromise as I didn't want to lose half my congregation by changing too much too quickly. Those who had become habituated to the all-singing, all-dancing folk Masses might find it hard to take if I changed everything in one fell swoop, so it seemed prudent to adopt a half-way solution at first. I would also bring in such forgotten things as incense and acolytes, assuming that I could find some altar servers. If all this went well and exhaustion didn't set in, I could then start to consider such dramatic possibilities as Benediction of the Blessed Sacrament and other such forgotten rites of the dim and distant past.

The second and third things still requiring attention were linked. The reordering had to be stopped, and this went hand in hand with the suppression of the Liturgy Planning Group. Given that I was preparing all the liturgy myself now, the latter had outrun its usefulness anyhow. While mulling all this over, I was interrupted by a phone call and found myself being addressed by none other than the bishop himself. Could I drive over and see him in Gorgehampton that afternoon? I could? How splendid. He would see me at three o'clock.

I had been expecting this summons for some time and had tried to prepare myself for it, but had no real clue as to what approach the bishop would take to the rumpus. If all that people said were true, he would be deeply opposed to everything I was doing and would try to put a stop to it. His secretary had, after all, previously tried to do just that. What would be my attitude if he did? Should I resign? It seemed the only honourable action. But what future would I then have in the diocese? It looked grim, especially if I ended up as the assistant to some modernist cleric in a trendy parish where I was forced to join in with all the things I had just got rid of at Cheeseminster. To cheer myself up, I decided to walk over to the school before lunch and have a chat with Julia about the textbooks. I found her teaching the same gang of halfwits she had been engaged with before.

'We're discussing confession, Father,' she said.

I was amazed.

'Is that in *Look At Me, Lord*?' I asked.

'No, but they seemed to want to talk about it.'

This was interesting. In my experience of the confessional in the parish so far, hardly any of the children appeared to use the sacrament and so I now decided to ask them why. I put the question directly to the peculiar-looking boy who had dominated the discussion last time and was greeted with a forthright response.

'Can't be bothered,' he said.

'Is that the only reason you don't go?'

'Can't see the point.'

I explained to him the point, asking if all this had been told him when he made his first confession a few years before.

'Can't remember,' he said.

This was getting tedious, so I explained to the group that regular confession was a very important practice, especially if they had committed a serious sin.

'Like what?' asked a girl at the back, who had perfected a posture advertising total contempt for the proceedings and who was, I was certain, concealing some gum in her mouth.

'Well,' I said, wondering what juicy sin to pick out of the bag. 'Like missing Mass.'

She seemed surprised that I thought this was serious.

'Me mum and dad don't go, so why should I?'

She had a point.

'Try to persuade them to go,' I said.

'Why don't you come round and tell them? You're the priest.'

I conceded the justice of this.

'What a good idea. Miss Anderson, please give me this girl's address after the lesson and I will visit her parents this week.'

The rest of the class seemed to think this was hilarious and the girl began to look embarrassed. I was content that I had at least made some kind of impact.

'Can you come round to our house?' said a untidy-looking boy with glasses.

'Yeh! And ours.'

Julia eventually got them to shut up again and I went off to the staff room for a cup of coffee. Later, she appeared and we went into our usual cupboard to discuss *Dogma And Doctrine*.

'Look,' she said, 'you've converted me. I'd like to use the book, but there are problems. First of all, we'd have to get the head to agree and she'd never do anything the educational committee wouldn't like. Secondly, there's the question of funding. I can't see her wanting to buy a whole new set of textbooks. I don't know what we can do.'

I told her to leave it to me, feeling that I might be able to talk the head round and willing, if necessary, to buy the textbooks out of my own pocket. In my years as an accountant I had managed to accumulate a fair amount of savings, especially from the sale of my house. Financially, there would be no problem. Immensely bucked by all this, I drove off to Gorgehampton, where I was greeted by the oily figure of Monsignor Rory Sloane.

I had never quite seen the point of Sloane, who had achieved some fame as a media priest and was even rumoured to be in the running for a slot on Radio Four's *Thought For The Day*. He now seemed to be a kind of spin-doctor for the bishop, the latter having retreated more and more into his office as the years had gone by and who now ventured out as little as possible. An imposing man, both by virtue of his height and bearing, Sloane was gifted with saturnine good looks and an ability to make everything in the diocese seem wonderful when it wasn't. Consequently the bishop, despite his sundry inadequacies, generally received a favourable press, both locally and in the national Catholic media. The two of them were made for each other, Sloane hailing from a distinguished convert family, while the bishop had formerly been headmaster of Windybacks, the prominent Catholic public school. All in all, they formed the lynchpin of the formidable liberal mafia that had dominated the diocese since the early eighties. Sloane waved me into the boss's inner sanctum.

'The bishop won't be long, James,' he said. 'He's just seeing to some paperwork. Would you like a sherry?'

We sat and talked of priests known in common until the bishop stepped into the room. A small man, wearing rimless spectacles, he had regular problems with his health that gave him an excuse for missing all kinds of official functions. Sloane usually deputised for him on these occasions. Sloane and I had stood up on his arrival, but with a wave of the hand we were ordered to seat ourselves again. After a certain amount of rummaging around with some files on his desk, the bishop made his way over and joined us where we had been sitting, the three chairs arranged in an intimate triangle as if to suggest that democratic processes were about to commence. I knew that was unlikely.

'Well, how are you, Jim?' asked the bishop, smiling broadly but failing to inject any warmth into it.

'Very well, thank you, bishop.'

'Been in the papers recently?'

'Oh, no, no, that's all calmed down again.'

'Good. I don't like it when these squabbles go public. I spoke to Lavender Buller afterwards and she agreed she may have gone a little far. Did you know that Lavender and Bernie are the godparents' of my sister's third child?'

I did not know this, but was not especially surprised. All these liberal troublemakers seemed to be related to each other. I reflected too that the Bullers' children had all passed through Windybacks when the bishop was headmaster there.

'Do you approve of We Are Right!, bishop?' I asked, wishing to get to the point of the discussion as quickly as possible. He seemed reluctant to answer and Sloane, as usual, helped him out.

'We Are Right! can be a little too vocal at times,' he said, in his customary, rather treacly manner, 'but they have a legitimate place among the voices that need to be heard in the diocese. I work closely with the Bullers and Miranda Phillips to make sure that nothing is said that could bring embarrassment to the diocese. Personally, I think many of their ideas are to be encouraged.'

The bishop nodded and I wondered whether WAR!'s constant calls for married and women priests had also been 'encouraged' by Sloane. Perhaps these were some of the areas where he agreed with them. I commented that Buller and Phillips had not exactly been helpful to me.

'Well, you did rather provoke them, didn't you, Jim?' said Sloane, shifting in his chair and glancing at the bishop. 'What on earth put it into to your head to make so many extraordinary changes without consulting them? It was bound to lead to trouble.'

'I'm the parish priest,' I replied. 'I don't see why I have to go along with people whose ideas are contrary to Catholic teaching. They have a completely wrong-headed view of 'Church', as they would call it. I'm convinced that I'm right.'

There was a long pause after this, and it seemed unclear for a moment which of them was going to take up the gauntlet. In the end, it was the bishop.

'I am sure, James,' he said, trying on the uneasy smile again, 'that you are passionate about what you're trying to do. In many ways your ideas are laudable and those of a more traditional disposition would no doubt approve of them. However, I have to stress that in my view the Church has moved on. Neo-traditionalism is simply not an option for our parishes in the post-Vatican II world. The Church is changing all the time and will soon begin to change even faster. With the shortage of priests, the laity will take on more and more jobs that the clergy used to do. People like Lavender Buller and Miranda Phillips are in many ways the future of the Church in this diocese, and I for one do not wish to antagonise them. You may have formed some views based on a reading of two or three rather traditionally-minded writers, but this is not the trend in the Church as a whole, especially not in this country. The current papacy may have encouraged some people to believe that the clock is being put back, but it is not. Very soon there will be a different Pope and things may move forward very quickly. I'm afraid there is simply no future for the kind of Church you are proposing.'

He sat back, evidently pleased that he had got this off his chest. There were so many things wrong with what he had said that I didn't know where to begin by way of response, so contented myself with saying that I disagreed with his diagnosis and thought that it was the diocese that was out of step, not the writers I had studied. It was Sloane who took up the baton.

'When did you last have a holiday, Jim?' he asked.
'In the summer.'

'And when did you take your retreat?'

'The same time as most of the other clergy – in July.'

'So you don't feel the need for a break?'

'Not at all. I'm just getting my teeth into things at Cheeseminster. Never felt better.'

The two of them shuffled in their chairs and I noticed a look passing between them. What did they have up their sleeves? It soon became clear. Apparently, a convent of enclosed nuns in the north of the diocese needed a chaplain for two weeks owing to the indisposition of the regular man. Furthermore, Sloane himself wanted to look more closely into the situation in Cheeseminster and would be happy to take on all normal duties in the parish while I was away. I felt like suggesting that it would be simpler if *he* went and looked after the nuns, but knew that I'd be wasting my time. If this was the price I would have to pay to remain at Cheeseminster, then so be it. I asked Sloane what he planned to do when I was away.

'We shall see,' he said. 'I shall talk informally to parishioners to see how they are taking the changes you have introduced. If it turns out that the views expressed by Greg Tonks and the Liturgy Planning Group are minority ones, then the situation can be reviewed. Neither the bishop nor myself would wish to oppose a parish priest in his work if it were proceeding smoothly. However, media interest has been aroused and it is important that nothing further is done to stir up the press. I'm sure you understand, Jim.'

I said that I understood.

'And,' said the bishop, beginning to look relaxed for the first time since the interview began, 'when you return, I can probably arrange for you to have some time at the Pastoral Centre. No doubt your views on the liturgy would be of great interest to the staff there and I'm sure they'd enjoy discussing them with you over a few beers.'

He began chuckling to himself, evidently highly relieved that not too much blood had been spilt during our little talk. I departed, feeling that things had gone better than expected, though unsure as to what Sloane's sojourn in the parish would ultimately mean for me. Of one thing I was certain: the real battle had only just begun.

NINE

The girl who had invited me round to discuss Mass attendance with her parents was called Leighanne Miller. I telephoned the number Julia Anderson had given me and arranged to see the family a few days later. They inhabited an estate in the town notorious for high levels of crime and general social disintegration, and my arrival turned out to be something of an event for the local residents, many of whom were sitting outside their houses, accompanied by their dogs and children, when I arrived. Leighanne herself was there, looking about eighteen years old in her home clothes and smelling of nicotine. I was introduced to her father, a large man, probably in his fifties, with an enormous belly and wearing a Gorgehampton Wanderers shirt. He grunted a bit when he saw me and asked if I wanted a beer.

    'No thanks, Mr. Miller.'

    'Cup of tea?'

    'That would be fine,' I said. 'Is Mrs. Miller with you?'

    'No. She's out with Jordan.'

    'Jordan?'

    'Our youngest.'

    'I don't think I know him.'

    'You wouldn't. He doesn't go to church.'

    This seemed a suitable moment to explain the purpose of my mission. Leighanne had come into the kitchen and listened as I explained the conversation we had had in the classroom. Miller now told her to make the tea while he opened a bottle of beer for himself. After he had taken a swig, he began to explain his reasons for non-attendance.

    'It's like this, Father,' he said. 'When I was a kid I was an altar server under Father Tillotson. Of course, he's dead now, but in those days all the Catholics round here used to go to Mass on Sunday. It was kind of expected. People just did it without thinking, or at least most of them did. A lot of us served the Mass, sometimes during the week as well. Then all the changes came along and gradually people stopped going. They didn't go to confession any more, either. None of the priests ever did anything about it. When Leighanne said you wanted to come round, I couldn't believe it. I went to the church a few years back when Leighanne had her First Communion, but it wasn't the same. That bloody idiot Greg Tonks was running the show and the priest just seemed to let him get on with it. He wasn't even wearing a collar. I thought to myself, why go along to a shambles like that? I haven't been back since.'

Leighanne passed me a cup of tea and disappeared to attend to more urgent tasks. I explained to Miller that I was trying to change things and asked him if he'd think about coming again. It wasn't, I explained, just a matter of whether he felt like it. Going to Mass was a serious obligation.

'Well,' he said, pondering the question. 'I might come once.'

Pleased to have wrung this out of him, I decided to press further.

'And what about confession?' I said. 'If you don't go, how can you expect the children to? You have to set an example.'

'You're right, Father, you're right.'

I left, wondering if I had really made any impact after all. He probably had other things he now did on a Sunday morning, and I knew only too well that once the regular habit of church attendance had fallen off, it was very difficult for people to get it back again. How many Millers had fallen away in the years since Vatican II, supposedly years of renewal and yet, as all the statistics showed, a disastrous period for the Church? My conviction was that, although this had something to do with the allurements of modern society drawing people away, it was much more on account of a perceived falling off by the Church from her previous certainties. In short, nobody believed any of it any more, including many of the priests.

On my return, I hurried into the church to see how many people had turned up for October Devotions. This, the daily, public recitation of the Rosary in the month dedicated to Our Lady, was another traditional practice I was determined to get off the ground, and I was gratified to see that a small number of the usual suspects had turned up to take part. I dedicated the first decade, the Annunciation, to the cause of spiritual renewal in the parish, wondering as I did so what I would find on my return from the convent two weeks later. Spooner was there, and I asked him afterwards how things were going with his search for a mate.

'I'm meeting someone next Tuesday in Chipping Knightly,' he said, cheerfully.

'Describe her to me.'

'She's a fun-loving blonde, twenty years old, who would like to meet an older man for games and frolics.'

This did not sound right at all.

'Are you sure this is wise?' I asked.

'Well, she looks good in the photo and she didn't waste any time when I suggested a date.'

'Are you sure she's a Catholic?'

'That's what she says.'

I pondered this.

'I'd go carefully if I were you, Mark. Do you know what she does for a living?'

'She was a bit vague about that.'

'Well, take it slowly. You could do without any further disasters at this stage.'

He agreed and I explained that I was soon going away for a fortnight and that he mustn't panic. However, he seemed so optimistic about his prospects with the blonde that he took the news in his stride.

The following Sunday I informed the two congregations of my imminent departure and also outlined the changes I was planning for my return. There was no sign of any of the Millers, so clearly I had been right in my gloomy prognosis of Mr. Miller's reactions. I wondered what had happened to my opponents in the WAR! camp, for none of them were to be seen at either Mass and I could only assume that they had pushed off to other parishes for the week-end. What little reaction I had to my announcements was mixed, but I felt that on the whole the level of dissent would be small. Increasingly, I was convinced that outside the WAR! faction there was little clamour for the practices I wanted to bury, and that in time the majority of parishioners would prefer a liturgy a bit more God-centred than they had been used to up to now. I learned that the lady who had offered to run a Gregorian choir was called Mrs. Moss, and speaking to me after Mass she agreed to begin recruiting singers for the ensemble while I was away. I also caught up with Drone and made arrangements for the first old rite Mass, to be celebrated on the Sunday after my return. Whatever might happen while I was at the convent, nothing, I felt, would get in my way once I got back. With Sloane out of my hair it would be full steam ahead, and if that meant losing the likes of Buller and Phillips, then so be it.

The convent of the Poor Clares at Sturton Newton turned out to be a delightful building in beautiful countryside. It also had a very good library, so, since my duties were light, I was able to catch up with some reading and generally recover from the events of the preceding month. Despite what I had told the bishop, a fortnight like this was very welcome and I now realised that I had been more battered by events than I realised. I resolved not to contact the parish and to try to treat the time as a retreat from the world. I also found that a couple of the older sisters were sympathetic to my views and encouraged me not to give up the fight. Assured of their prayers, I returned home refreshed and ready for the fray. My equanimity lasted only as long as my first conversation with Sloane.

'How are things?' I asked, meeting him in the kitchen on my arrival.

'I'm enjoying myself,' he replied, managing to look smug and shifty at the same time. 'You have a wonderful parish community here, James.'

'I'm pleased you think so.'

'Oh, yes. The first thing I have to tell you is that Greg Tonks is out of hospital.'

'How splendid,' I said, unable to put much conviction into it.

'In fact,' continued Sloane, 'he's so much recovered that he was able to run the choir again at last week's eleven o'clock Mass.'

'Really?'

'Yes, he's back in harness. Everyone is delighted.'

I was speechless. For a start, I had assumed that Tonks, judging by what he himself had told me, would be ill for much longer than that. Furthermore, I wondered what had happened about Mrs. Moss.

'Oh, you mean the lady who wants to start a Gregorian chant choir?' said Sloane, when I brought this up. 'I told her to speak to you about it when you got back. She seemed to understand how things stood, especially since Tonks' choir clearly has the prior claim.'

I couldn't believe what I was hearing. I had made a definite promise to the poor woman, and the wretched Sloane had now told her to go and take a running jump. Well, I wasn't going to stand for this. As soon as Sloane packed his bags and returned to Gorgehampton, I would make sure that Tonks understood that he was no longer required. This was tiresome in the extreme, but it seemed that another confrontation with the bearded wonder would be inevitable. Sloane, however, was not finished yet.

'You'll also be delighted to hear,' he said, pouring me a cup of tea, 'that the liturgy talks have continued. Bernie Buller gave us a most fascinating couple of hours on liturgical renewal in today's Church. He was able to show, I think, that a more pastorally orientated liturgy is nothing to be afraid of. I think some of the older members of the audience had been slightly misled by a few things Canon Taylor said and were interested to hear a more up-to-date perspective.'

'I bet they were,' I said, unable to think of any adequate comment.

This was annoying and I wished I'd been there to chair the meeting. The poor old dears must be more confused than ever now and it would be difficult to clear up the resulting mess. I waited to hear more of what Sloane had been up to. There was plenty of it.

'Then there's the matter of the Latin Masses,' he continued, the smugness beginning to get the upper hand of the shiftiness. 'Now, despite a thorough grounding in the Classics at my public school, I really didn't feel up to dusting off *Kennedy's Latin Primer* this time around and so decided to use the English translations. No-one seemed to mind.'

This didn't surprise me. I hadn't expected for a moment that a dyed-in-the-wool liberal like Sloane would say Mass in Latin, and so took this piece of news in my stride. He was, however, saving the biggest shock to last. I asked him when he was planning to bring his stay to a close.

'There's no hurry for me to be off,' he said, with a grin. 'In fact, the bishop told me last night that he'd like me to help you a little while longer. We can sort things out together.'

I nearly spilt my tea.

'Are you sure he said that?' I spluttered.

'Quite sure.'

'So when will you leave?'

'When the bishop is sure that all is well here and that you've settled in comfortably. The precise timescale for that is, in the end, entirely up to you.'

All was now clear. If I toed the party line and did as they wanted, Sloane would be off my back within the week. If I did not, he would hang around until I gave in, perhaps sending me to the pastoral centre for good measure to be re-educated in modernist doctrines. I asked him if he could really afford the time.

'Of course I can, James,' he replied. 'This is an important parish for the diocese. In many respects it could be a model for the future, especially with so many committed laypeople working here. Tonight, by the way, I thought it might be a good idea for the Liturgy Planning Group to meet. They'll be here in about an hour, so I suppose you'll be wanting to get on with your meal.'

This was very bad news indeed.

'What about you?' I asked.

'I've already eaten.'

How much ghastlier could things get? My house had been invaded by Lord Snooty, I had been backed into a corner from which it was going to be very difficult to get myself out and Lavinia Buller was on the march again. The thought of an imminent Liturgy Planning Group meeting was all I needed to round off a perfect nightmare of a day.

As they trooped in, I felt more depressed than at any time since taking up my post in the parish. Needless to say, my chief enemies made a point of ignoring me and the whole meeting was conducted through Sloane. The only consolation was that Julia had turned up and was voted onto the group, being warmly welcomed by Sloane in his oiliest manner. A brisk discussion of the eleven o'clock Mass established that it would be business as usual, with O'Grady evidently back in harness as well. Fortunately, Sloane offered to preside and attention was now turned to the eight o'clock. Phillips deigned to bring me into the discussion for the first time.

'Will James be saying the eight o'clock, Rory?' she asked, not condescending to look in my direction.

'How do you feel about that, Jim?' asked Sloane, the oil practically dripping from him.

'Well,' I said, trying to sound as sarcastic as possible. 'I think I would be a little under-employed if I said neither of the two Sunday Masses.'

Sloane agreed that this was so. However, he immediately added the rider that he did not feel that now was the time to introduce Latin at the Mass. It would only, he said, cause further confusion, especially as Bernie Buller had stressed the importance of vernacular Masses in his talk only a few days ago.

'I agree,' cut in Phillips, 'I really don't think a Latin Mass on a Sunday is appropriate here. What do other people think?'

Tonks and O'Grady were quick to back her up and Mouse One, whom I had now learned to call by her real name of Mavis Bird, said nothing to contradict them. Mouse Two, however, who was in fact her sister, actually went so far as to speak up in my favour. She boldly stated that she enjoyed the Latin Masses on weekdays and thought that they would go down well on Sundays too. Buller and Phillips ignored such heresy, while Sloane thanked her politely for her views. The patronising note in his voice as he did so was unmistakeable. At this point, however, Julia chose to speak up. She had previously seemed a little nervous in such high-powered company, but now came out strongly in my favour. The consternation from the Buller/Phillips axis was immediately apparent.

'But you can't want a Latin Mass,' said Phillips, while Buller looked at Julia as if she had suddenly taken leave of her senses. 'Why, you can't be more that twenty-five. What possible appeal can it hold for you?'

Julia explained that, not only had she been convinced by my and Canon Taylor's arguments and unconvinced by Bernie Buller, she also found the Latin Mass more prayerful and mysterious than its vernacular equivalent. She even went so far as to say that she had read some of Cardinal Schmidt's book and been impressed by his arguments. Buller now cut in.

'Perhaps you ought to read my husband's book, *All Together Now*. That will put you right. I am upset by your views, Julia, very upset. Young people today do not want a return to the past and you, as a teacher, should realise that.'

It was evident that she was right behind Sloane in her wish to patronise any opponents of the cultural revolution, but I could see that Julia had not been impressed by being treated

92

like this. However, when it came to a vote the liberals easily won the day and I was forced by Sloane to agree to continuing with the English Mass, at least for the present. I wondered if anything would be said about the altar rails, but this did not appear to be on the agenda.

The discussion moved to the weekday Masses, and Sloane declared that he wished to take charge of his fair share of these. I said that I was quite prepared to continue saying them all, but he brushed this aside, arguing that if he was going to be resident in the parish for a while it was only right that he should do an honest week's work. It did not take very long for it to be established that these Masses would be said in English, while I could continue to say mine in Latin. Buller chipped in again.

'Will you continue saying your Mass with your back to the congregation?' she asked venomously, throwing a glance in Sloane's direction. 'I really do not see how this can be justified any longer.'

'If you come to one of my Masses, you'll find out,' I said.

Sloane moved in to break up this quarrel.

'I am sure James must do as he sees fit. While some of us may have different views on this matter, we should respect his position.'

It was good to know that I was not going to be humiliated too far and that Sloane knew where to draw the line. Buller was clearly not satisfied, but she chose to say nothing further. Under the heading of Other Business, I informed the group that I had agreed to say a monthly Sunday Mass at three o'clock for the Campaign for Real Catholicism. Phillips had clearly heard nothing of this.

'You do realise,' she said, 'that you must have permission from the bishop to do that. Who put you up to it?'

As usual, I didn't like her tone, but decided to answer the question.

'Hubert Drone has cleared it with the bishop. Compared with most other dioceses, the CRC here gets granted very few old rite Masses and the monthly Mass in Cheeseminster will merely be a continuation of the one that used to happen at Muckford. You may object, but it's been agreed.'

She was clearly not happy.

'I really don't think that this parish should be associated with something like that,' she said.

She made it sound a really disgraceful activity, on a par with ritual murder or child abuse. Fortunately, Sloane once again showed a grasp of *realpolitik*.

'James is right, Lavinia. The bishop has agreed to it.'

'Then it's about time I had another chat with him.'

I almost began to feel sorry for his Lordship, and I could see that even Sloane was beginning to be a little weary of Phillips' constant carping.

Finally, the meeting broke up, Buller informing Sloane that she would ensure that next time the buffet would be resumed, and people began to take their leave. Julia caught me before she went.

'I'm so sorry, Father,' she said, squeezing my arm.

It almost made it all worthwhile.

(TEN)

The evening, however, turned out not to be over yet. As I
ushered the Mice, or, I should say, the Birds out, I caught sight
of Mark Spooner deep in conversation with Julia about
halfway down the drive. My first thought was one of terror
that he had come for a late-night chat about his love life and I
was right.

    'Can't it wait until tomorrow?' I said.

    'No. I need to go to confession.'

    'Oh.'

    Once we had got that over with, he unburdened
himself in some detail about his encounter with the fun-loving
blonde. As usual, his naivety had set the tone for the evening.

    'When she turned up at the pub,' he said, 'I couldn't
believe my eyes. She was really attractive and was wearing an
incredibly short skirt.'

    'I don't need to hear all the details,' I said. 'Just stick
to the essentials.'

    'Right, sorry, Father. Anyway, we chatted for a bit
and got through quite a lot of drinks pretty quickly. Then she
began to paw me and ruffle my hair and I couldn't believe my
luck. The next thing I knew she'd invited me round to her
place.'

    This was a far from promising start.

    'What was her name?' I asked.

    'Fifi LaPlage.'

    He didn't really need to tell me the rest, but I let him
carry on.

    'As soon as we got there she dragged me up to her
bedroom and began to take my clothes off. It was then that I
became suspicious. I asked her what she was doing and said
that I had not expected a girl who advertised with the Internet
Catholic Dating Agency to be quite so up for it - if you'll

excuse the expression, Father. She then started going on about how Catholics were no different from anybody else and that a lot of business had come her way through that particular website. It was then that I clicked what was going on.'

He paused, as if conjuring up the astonishing scene once again.

'Now, this is where you will be really pleased with me,' he continued, gulping at his words a little. 'Despite finding her very attractive and already having had quite a few beers, I told her that I was one Catholic who had a little more respect for the teachings of the Church. I said I didn't do this sort of thing and that I would now be taking my leave. I was down the stairs and out onto the road in a flash.

He paused again.

'What do you think about that, Father?'

It was hard to think of an adequate comment.

'Well,' I said, at last. 'At least it shows you can resist your urges when money comes into it. Have you informed the dating agency of the cuckoo they have in their nest?'

'No,' he replied. 'I hadn't thought of that.'

'Well, perhaps you'd better. I don't think Miss LaPlage is exactly the sort of woman they would want their clients to meet.'

I offered him a beer, amazed once more at his capacity to choose exactly the wrong person for an evening out. I asked him if he had been put off by his recent experiences.

'Yes, I have actually,' he said. 'In fact, that's what I was talking to Julia Anderson about just before I came in this evening.'

'You told her about Fifi LaPlage?' I said, horrified.

'Well, not in so many words. But she got the gist of it. I like Julia very much, Father. Do you think she'd be interested if I asked her out?'

I nearly choked on my beer. The idea was too preposterous for words.

'Look, Mark,' I said, trying to find a nice way of saying it, 'don't even think about it. I've told you before, Julia has a boyfriend. She is out of bounds.'

'Not any more,' he said, looking rather pleased with himself.

'What do you mean?'

'They've split up. You remember that time she turned up here without her car? Well, they'd had a row and he'd driven off somewhere. It turned out that he was seeing someone else.'

This was all news to me, but I had to assume it was true. However, I still felt it was my duty to keep Spooner off Julia's back. The last thing she would want in the wake of a shock like Ray's infidelity was Spooner ringing her up at every hour of the day or night. I explained all this to him in words of one syllable, but had the feeling that it wasn't really going in. The next disaster, I sensed, was already looming on the horizon and I would no doubt soon be the recipient of yet another tale of woe.

The following morning, Sloane was up bright and early to say Mass and I decided to slip into the back of the church to see what approach he would take. It was worse than I could possibly have imagined. The first thing that greeted my eyes was a spanking new cardboard altar, more horrible, if that were possible, than the one I had destroyed. Sloane was sitting facing the congregation in what he would probably have called the 'president's chair', engaging them in a discussion on what it meant to be 'Church' in the modern world. The few old biddies who had bothered to turn up were yawning away and I could tell that it was not going down well. It would be interesting to see how many of them would reappear the next day, especially if it was made clear that Latin would once again be on the agenda.

Deprived of saying a public Mass, I decided to say a private one just as soon as Sloane had gone off for his toast and cereals. I wanted to get some much needed practice at saying the old rite Mass, so opted to use this one. One thing that had become immediately apparent was that I would have to try to learn by heart the psalm which preceded the Mass and which had been cut when the new rite was cooked-up in the sixties. There were also a number of other formulae that would have to be mastered if I were not to make a complete hash of things on Sunday. No doubt Canon Taylor, despite his years, had been a slick operator in this area, and I didn't want the members of the CRC to think that I couldn't be bothered to get it right.

The Mass over, I went off to get some breakfast and found Sloane knocking the top off a boiled egg. The remains of a large breakfast were spread around him and I was beginning to see how he had acquired his impressive physique.

'Ah, James,' he said, moving across the kitchen to get me some coffee, 'I trust you slept well?'

I answered in the affirmative.

'Good, because we must tackle the question of the reordering.'

I thought this was a pretty low blow, to bring up something so fundamental to my whole future in the parish before I had even eaten breakfast, but steeled myself to parry whatever nonsense he was preparing to spout. He informed me that while I was away he had held a meeting of the parish council and it had been agreed that there would be a public meeting in the hall to display the plans for the reordering and allow people to give their views. I expressed my annoyance that he had not waited for my return before organising something of this importance.

'I'm sorry, James,' he said, not looking as if he meant it, 'but one of the tasks the bishop has given me is to bring this issue to a speedy conclusion before I leave. Since all the plans are ready and the scheme has been thoroughly costed, there is no need to wait any longer. Time is of the essence.'

I asked him what he thought of the scheme and he paused before answering, evidently wishing to choose his words carefully.

'I am aware that you yourself are not in favour of the plan,' he said eventually, 'and that you see no merit in this kind of reordering. However, I really must beg to differ. The demands of a truly dynamic and pastoral liturgy today mean that we must grasp the opportunity to order our churches in ways that reflect these changes. The church here has been barely touched since the seventies, apart from the introduction of the new altar, and is ripe for redevelopment. If we are going to do it, which we must, it ought to be done properly. As it stands, the church is hardly an architectural gem, and I think that in many ways the reordering will help to make it one.'

He gave me a long, intense stare, as if willing me to agree with him. I still felt it was too early in the morning to embark on a full scale discussion of something like this, but now, for the umpteenth time, I tried to get him to see why I was opposed to the plan. Who, I said, were demanding these changes? Who had decreed that a large baptismal pool, wall-to-wall carpeting and an altar in the centre of the church were required for the celebration of the liturgy? These were merely passing fads, dreamed up by people with too much time on their hands and without precedent in church architecture in the whole western tradition. A moment's reflection would surely make him see that he was the victim of a trend that would need to be reversed at some point in the not too distant future when more orthodox ideas began to take hold again.

I immediately realised I had gone too far. It only now hit me that Sloane was a true believer, the possessor of a messianic urge to bring change to the Church at whatever cost. To him, my ideas were tantamount to blasphemy. As a founder of the pastoral centre, an intimate of the Bullers and a fully signed-up modernist, he could not possibly tolerate the utterance in his presence of an alternative creed. For a moment, he looked as if he would rise up and smite me, but then his ire appeared to calm and I saw him quietly taking up a spoonful of boiled egg. I wondered whether he would ever deign to speak to me again. However, we were saved from further discussion by the arrival of none other than Terry Molloy. I invited him in for some breakfast.

'A cup of tea wouldn't hurt,' he said, as if speaking from the depths of a primeval fog. 'I'm not used to doing the dawn patrol.'

He slouched into the house and I asked him what had caused him to rise from his slumbers at such an unearthly hour.

'I had to take my dear old mum to Bristol Airport,' he said. 'Truly a Hell on earth.'

When he entered the kitchen and saw Sloane he practically jumped backwards, unable to cope with any further assaults on his equilibrium. I remembered now that Sloane had had an obscure part in Terry's fall from grace all those years ago and that the two of them were far from the best of friends. After a curt greeting, he sat down and brought up the reason for his visit.

'I've been on the blower to the Beast,' he said.

'Who?'

'Dermot Byrne, remember, the Beast of Chedderford. He's arranged for Petroc Tomkinson to come and give a talk for you in your liturgy series. You're very lucky to get him, Jim. I think,' he said, giving Sloane a significant look, 'he'd heard what's going on here and was anxious to help out.'

Sloane did not take this well. In fact, he looked as though he'd been possessed by the Dark Side again and I thought he might be about to pronounce some anathema upon us. Terry was clearly enjoying the effect he was creating and now named a date for the talk in early November. I could see Sloane desperately trying to think of ways of countering this.

'Is this wise?' he said, finally beginning to regain his composure. 'Would it not be better to bring these talks to a close now? Bernie Buller has, I think, succeeded brilliantly in summing up the issues, and to reopen the debate again would simply confuse people further.'

'Too late,' cut in Molloy, clearly pleased to have a chance to deflate his old enemy. 'Tomkinson's coming and I wouldn't advise upsetting him. He's a great pal of Gerald Nutter.'

I could see these words had made an impact. Nutter, as Sloane would know only too well, was the rather off-message editor of the *Catholic Mercury*, and, from what had been said at our meeting in Gorgehampton, it was clear the bishop was determined to avoid any further media interest in the events at Cheeseminster. The party broke up with Sloane looking less than pleased by what had transpired and I wondered how he would take his revenge.

It did not take long for me to find out. Somehow or other, Sloane had got wind of my plans for the eviction of *Look At Me, Lord* from the school. I think he had been nosing around there during my absence and Julia, unaware of his diabolical tendencies, must have let something slip about our plans. What made things worse was that Sloane had been on the consultative body that had formed *Look At Me, Lord* in the first place.

'Quite simply,' he told me a few days after our breakfast chat, 'we do not do *Dogma and Doctrine* in this diocese. The education committee, of which I am chair, made up our minds about this some time ago, and the introduction of such a textbook would not be countenanced. You may think you can do just what you like in this parish, James, but you've still got an awful lot to learn.'

I thought this was a bit rich, given everything that had happened, but said nothing. With Sloane firmly established in the presbytery, it was clearly not going to be possible to make any further progress on this issue in the immediate future. I therefore decided to keep my head down for a bit and concentrate on preparing for Sunday afternoon and the old rite Mass. At two-thirty on the day in question, after a protracted lunch during which Sloane had favoured me with reminiscences of his days at the English College in Rome, I turned up to find Drone fully kitted-up in cassock and cotta and putting out the altar cards. He had removed Sloane's new portable monstrosity and seemed happy in his work, being especially pleased with the altar rails.

'We didn't have these at Muckford,' he said. 'This is a vast improvement. Also, the church is bigger. I see a great deal of potential here, so I'll be interested to see how many people we get today. Three o'clock in the afternoon isn't a good time, but the membership is growing because people are getting more and more fed up with the modern Masses. We even get quite a few young people now.'

I had noticed that attendance at the eight o'clock was down a little this week and wondered whether some of the regulars would attend this Mass instead. As I stared at the sanctuary to see whether Drone had forgotten anything, my eye was suddenly caught by the fact that one of the altar rails was slightly askew. Upon examining it I found that it was no longer attached to the floor and that somebody had evidently moved it. Of course, it was obvious what was going on. Without telling me, Sloane had decreed that he had no use for the rails at the eleven o'clock Mass and had arranged for O'Grady to remove them. If they had been put back in better order, I might never have noticed that they had been moved at all. At least, I reflected, they had not been destroyed altogether.

In time, a steady trickle of people began to arrive and the church was at least a third full by the time the Mass commenced. I had dug out a suitably dignified-looking chasuble and had donned a biretta that Canon Taylor had found for me at the convent. It turned out that he had saved quite a bit of ecclesiastical bric-a-brac like this, waiting for the day when the vandals had passed away and order would be restored. All in all, the Mass went well. I remembered most of my lines and Drone and his two assistants turned out to be efficient servers, helping me through the difficult bits and ringing the bell at the right moments. At the end of the Mass, they expressed their amazement that I had been able to learn the rubrics so quickly and I went out to chat to the departing faithful in a better humour than I had been in for days.

Many of the people outside the church were complete strangers to me, refugees from other parishes who had driven miles to get their monthly fix of the old rite. Mrs. Moss was there too and I was able to explain to her how things stood with regard to the Gregorian Chant choir. She told me not to worry about it.

'I'm thinking of setting up the choir anyway,' she said. 'If you're amenable, we could sing at one of these traditional rite Masses. I'd prefer that anyway. What do you think?'

I raised no objection, and when she had moved off had a word with Julia and Spooner who had, rather disturbingly, arrived together. It turned out that Spooner's car had broken down again and that Julia had returned the favour of a lift.

'We thought we'd like to support you today, Father,' she said. 'I must say, I found this Mass rather different from the one you do during the week. Why did you go all quiet during the Eucharistic Prayer?'

I explained the mysteries of the silent Canon, and told her that it had not been customary for the priest to speak out loud during that part of the Mass under the former dispensation. During this discussion, Spooner kept his eyes fixed on Julia like a dog waiting for a stick to be thrown, and only became animated when she asked him if he would like a lift back.

'Why don't we go for a drink first?' he said.

'Oh, yes,' said Julia. 'What a good idea. Are you free now, Father? We could go to that pub across the road.'

I wasn't sure about this suggestion. So far, I had avoided the establishment across from the church, rather a rough-looking dive that seemed exactly the sort of place where the Nurdles might perform. However, I agreed, feeling that a pint might not go amiss. Furthermore, it was a bright October day and I suggested we sit in the beer garden at the back.

'Why not?' said Julia, looking prettier today than ever and making Spooner, up against her, look like an actor auditioning for a part in *Beauty and the Beast*. We crossed the road and, after buying drinks in an almost deserted bar, seated ourselves in the garden. Julia now began to tell me about her split from Ray while Spooner listened avidly. From what she said it seemed that nothing could save the relationship and that Ray, whom I had previously put down as rather a good chap, had been deceiving her for a long time. I told her he was a fool, a comment that elicited several furious nods from Spooner, who now offered to return to the bar and buy another round. After he disappeared, Julia began to quiz me about Sloane and, made eloquent by the beer, I started to give her the full picture.

'But this is terrible,' she said, after listening carefully to what I had to say. 'I really don't like that Lavender Buller woman, you know. I'm sure she's behind all this. I bet she gave some kind of ultimatum to the bishop. Do you think maybe she's trying to squeeze you out?'

'I'm sure of it.'

'So what are you going to do?'

'I really don't know. The critical thing is the reordering. If that goes ahead, I'm not certain I could put up with things here any more. I'd feel that I'd tried to take a stand and been defeated in my own parish.'

She thought about this for a bit.

'But can't you just chuck the scheme out?' she said.

'In theory, yes, I could. But everything has become so political here now, I don't think that that's an option any more, especially if the public meeting goes against me. With Sloane calling the shots and the bishop backing him, I haven't really got much room for manoeuvre.'

Her sympathetic attitude cheered me and I was glad to have so fervent an ally. Spooner now returned from the bar but continued to say little, merely sipping nervously at his beer and donning a pair of sunglasses that made him look like an underfed gangster. Not long afterwards, I suddenly noticed Mr. Miller strolling into the garden, accompanied by a large dog. He waved and approached our table.

104

'Don't tell the missus, Father,' he said. 'She thinks I'm working overtime.'

I asked him to join us, but he said he'd only come out of the pub for a breath of fresh air. Julia and Spooner now took their leave, but rather than going with them I decided to tackle Miller about his non-appearance at any of my Masses. To give him his due, he seemed a little embarrassed.

'Well, it's like this, Father,' he said. 'I've been a bit busy recently. I tell you what - I'll come next week.'

I asked him whether he was generally free on a Sunday afternoon and, grinning, he said he normally slipped off to the pub to escape the hubbub of family life. An idea now struck me.

'I'll make you a promise,' I said. 'If you come next month to the Mass I do at three o'clock, I'll buy you a drink afterwards.'

'Sounds reasonable, Father,' he replied. 'O.K, you've got yourself a deal.'

'Shake on it?'

He nodded.

With our agreement fixed, I moved off, pleased to have got him on side. I wondered whether I should tell Sloane about my conversations with Miller, but decided against. Somehow I felt he didn't really care who came to Mass, so long as things were done in an ideologically acceptable manner, and he certainly wouldn't have worried about one of the great unwashed like Miller. On my return I found him deep into a copy of *Reordering Monthly* and, resisting the urge to ask him if that was how often things now had to be done, left him to it.

ELEVEN

The following day being my day off, I decided to go for a stroll in the town and no sooner had I stepped into the market square than I bumped into a man in a dog-collar sporting a panama hat. It was, of course, none other than my old university chum, Spencer White, now Anglican vicar of Cheeseminster. Although never exactly great friends, we had vaguely kept in contact over the years, but since arriving in the town I had not got around to paying him a call and our paths had never crossed. He greeted me warmly.

'I've been away,' he said, when I enquired as to his movements. 'A late holiday. When I got back, one of my parishioners told me about the shenanigans going on at your church. What on earth have you been up to?'

I explained the trials I was undergoing.

'So you've got a minder, have you?' he said, clearly concerned though also, perhaps, a little amused by these developments. 'No doubt he'll be frightfully keen on that dreadful Churches Together group we all have to go to from time to time. Has he told you about the service he's arranged for the end of the month?'

I knew nothing of this.

'Service? What service?'

'A sort of ecumenical thing. Dancing nuns and so forth. The Salvation Army playing their tambourines and everyone agreeing that we all love one another really and that all differences will soon be wiped out. Anthea's very keen on it.'

'Who's Anthea?'

'My number two. Why not come and meet her?'

We weren't far from the Minster, so I went into the porch with him and noticed a rather dippy-looking woman in a clerical collar pinning up a notice on the board. Her hair was cut in a curious bob, which gave her the effect of wearing a highly-burnished helmet, and she had the most enormous front teeth. Spencer explained who I was and I thought for a moment she was going to burst into a fit of giggles.

'I've just told Father Page about the ecumenical service,' said Spencer. 'He knew nothing about it.'

The woman's eyes popped open a little larger at this, as if she were highly surprised at my ignorance of this important project.

'But, Father,' she said. 'I left a message on your answer phone several weeks ago. Didn't you get it?'

'No, I didn't,' I said.

'Well, it doesn't matter because Monsignor Sloane rang me and arranged everything. You do realise that it's the biggest Churches Together event of the year? We've even managed to get the Sisters of Servitude to team up with the Nuns of the Paraclete to perform some liturgical dance together. Our choirmaster has written the music for it. It's going to be super.'

I wasn't happy about any of this. For a start, like Spencer, I didn't really approve of these ecumenical jamborees and, while quite happy to be friendly with my clerical counterparts, did not really see the need to hold services with them. As for the Nuns of the Paraclete, I knew only that they were a group quite as dotty as our own Sisters, but with the advantage that they were Anglican and therefore outside my jurisdiction.

We left Anthea to continue her work on the notice-board and Spencer and I stepped outside again. He sympathised with me on my plight and said that he hoped Sloane would soon be off my back.

'Is that ridiculous reordering scheme going ahead?' he asked.

'There's a meeting coming up about it very soon.'

'Goodness knows,' he remarked, 'your church isn't exactly beautiful, but there's no need to go down that road.

Will you be expected to baptise people by full immersion if you have a pool?'

'I suppose so.'

He smiled broadly at this and I felt embarrassed for my own Church. Why did we come up with all the loony schemes these days? That was supposed to be the job of the Anglicans. At this we parted, Spencer expressing the hope that I might forgo my principles and come along to the ecumenical service, if only so that we could have a few laughs together. He promised that the Nuns of the Paraclete would not disappoint me.

The next week or so passed without major incident and life took on its new pattern. In many ways the arrangement I had sorted out with Sloane worked well and I was particularly grateful not to have to have any involvement with the eleven o'clock Mass. I reflected that things might not have been too bad if our two ideologies could have existed side by side, but I knew that this was merely the calm before the storm, a temporary respite before all Hell was let loose at the reordering meeting. The day for this crept ever closer, and I made sure that I was always present at the daily October Devotions, praying desperately for some kind of reprieve from the calamity to come. Amazingly, Sloane had allowed these devotions to continue, despite making a point of telling me in private that he thought the Rosary a childish prayer fit only for the weak of intellect. When I pointed out that the present Pontiff had proclaimed it his favourite prayer and that sundry Popes in the past had heaped praise on it, he merely laughed and walked off. Somehow, I felt, he didn't put great store by the pronouncements of the Roman Pontiffs, and I wondered whether he thought some imminent ecumenical dawn was about do away with the need for them.

By a quirk of Providence that I shall always look back on as the fruit of my prayers, the date designated for Dr. Petroc Tomkinson's talk turned out to be the very evening before the reordering meeting. Beforehand, I was anxious that, faced with too many meetings in one week, parishioners might be inclined to skip the Tomkinson one and keep their powder dry for the latter. I therefore made sure that maximum publicity was generated for the coming of our tame celebrity liturgist and urged Terry Molloy to do the same. Fortunately, Hubert Drone agreed to give the talk a full page advertisement in his monthly letter to members of the CRC and I was able to get something slipped into the *Cheeseminster Echo*. When Sloane spotted this he was not best pleased.

'I thought we were trying to keep out of the papers,' he said, on seeing the article.

'But this is *good* news.'

He did not comment further. The day before the meeting I received an unexpected phone call before Mass.

'Beast here,' said a voice.

'Who?'

'Dermot Byrne. Known to everyone as the Beast of Chedderford.'

'Oh, Father Byrne. Hello.'

'Don't worry,' he continued in a deep, rather gravelly voice, 'I'm bringing a coach-load of my parishioners down to Tomkinson's talk to support you. Told them they had to come.'

'Good.'

'Molloy going to be there?'

'Yes.'

'Canon Taylor?'

'No, he's too ill after his operation.'

'I suppose the wretched Bernie Buller's turning up? Still, no problem there. We'll make mincemeat of him, eh?'

'I sincerely hope so.'

'Good. See you tomorrow.'

He rang off and Sloane was surprised to encounter me a little later whistling on my way across to the church. I was now saying the old rite Mass in private on a regular basis, having made sure through the bishop's office that there was no barrier to my doing so. I knew how touchy people could be about it, but since I had evidently been written off as a lunatic whose days would soon be numbered anyway, no objection was made. Now that I was becoming more comfortable with the Mass, I could begin to appreciate its extraordinary beauty and see why Drone and his acolytes were so keen on it. Although the latter had expressed his appreciation of the new rite Latin Mass when I had introduced it, I could see that he regarded it as a pale imitation of the real thing and now knew why he had remained determined that I should take on the old rite. The prayers it contained, I had discovered, were genuinely ancient in most cases, and the whole thing had the feel of a distillation of wisdom passed down through the ages, the fruit of centuries of sacrifice and worship. The new Latin Mass, on the other hand, had the marks of being exactly what it was, the product of a hastily assembled liturgical cabal. I was reminded of the old adage that a camel was a horse designed by a committee, and there was a world of difference between the lumbering, if serviceable vehicle of the new rite and the graceful beauty of the old. It seemed that here we were confronted with yet another example of modern man thinking he could tear up the work of centuries in an instant and suddenly replace it with something better. The new rite Mass proved once again that he couldn't.

TWELVE

Apparently, Petroc Tomkinson couldn't drive, so it fell to me to pick him up at the station. After his train pulled in I was soon confronted by a small, rather dapper man of indeterminate age in a mackintosh and trilby hat. I asked him if he'd had a pleasant journey.

He looked at me as if I were mad.

'By no means,' he said, rather testily. 'There was no buffet on the train and I missed lunch. I hope you have something edible lined up for me back at the presbytery.'

'Well, no, actually,' I said. 'I thought we'd go out for a curry.'

The suggestion clearly appalled him.

'I do not eat curry,' he said, emphatically. 'Besides, the odour would hardly be an attractive one to carry into the meeting. No, no, you must cook me something yourself.'

His tone brooked no refusal and as we drove off I tried to make a mental audit of what we had in the freezer. I asked him if he liked fish fingers.

'Never having eaten them, Father Page, I would not know. No, what I would like is a hearty steak or something. Perhaps you could fry me some chips.'

This was beginning to sound better. Steak and chips could not be too difficult to produce and I felt certain that I had the wherewithal to do so. I knew that Sloane, quite a passable cook, would be no use. He had already told me that he was going out for an early dinner and would not turn up until the commencement of the talk. It was clearly up to me to prepare the meal myself.

Tomkinson had expressed a desire to stay the night, so I showed him up to the spare room. Once again, he seemed less than satisfied with the arrangements made for him.

'Why is there no bedside light?' he asked, accusingly.

'I don't know,' I said. 'I'll fix you one up later.'

'But I want it now.'

'Before dinner?'

'Yes. It is dreadfully dark in here and I wish to go over my talk.'

I returned with the lamp from my own room and went off to prepare the meal. Fortunately, there were indeed two frozen steaks in the house and I discovered some prefabricated chips that would only take a few minutes in the fryer. The steaks could be defrosted in the microwave prior to cooking. So far, so good, then. It then occurred to me that I didn't know how Tomkinson liked his steak, but, loath to interrupt him in his preparations for the talk, I laid the table and waited until he came down. He appeared some half an hour later, wearing a sombre suit and a striped bow tie.

'Is everything ready?' he asked.

'Well, I've fried the chips,' I said.

'Good.'

'But I wasn't sure how you liked your steak.'

'Rare,' he said, decidedly, 'very rare. Barely touch the pan with the meat, but make sure the oil is hot enough before you do so. The oil must be very hot, do you hear? Very, very hot.'

I began to hope that the talk, when it came, would be good enough to make up for the nuisance of having this fellow around. The Beast of Chedderford had not explained that Tomkinson was some kind of arch fusspot and I did not welcome having such a difficult guest. I began to heat the oil.

'Some wine, Doctor?' I asked, tentatively.

'Of course not,' he moaned. 'How do expect me to deliver my talk if I've been drinking? I sometimes think you clergy live entirely out of the world.'

I put the bottle away, feeling unable to drink anything if he refused to do so. This was annoying, as I was counting on a few glasses of wine to steady my nerves. We now sat uneasily at the table as the oil gradually heated up. At every moment I wondered whether the time had come to plunge the steaks in, but was reluctant to make a move that could be criticised as premature. Eventually Tomkinson practically shouted, 'Well, get on with it! We don't want a fire,' and I quickly got to my feet, seizing the larger of the two steaks as I did so. In a flash, I had it in the pan.

'Turn it over now,' shouted Tomkinson above all the spitting. 'Don't you have any cutlery?'

I realised I had forgotten to take out a spatula that could be used to turn the steak over and now hurriedly began to search in the usual draw. Not a single suitable implement was to be seen.

'Turn it over!' shouted Tomkinson again.

'I'm trying, Doctor.'

'No you're not. You're just fiddling around in that draw. *You'll* have to have that one now. It will be far too well done for me.'

Eventually I found what I was looking for and put aside the steak for myself. As quickly as was humanly possible I turned the second one over and Tomkinson pronounced himself satisfied. We now ate a grim meal, my guest seemingly disinclined to strike up any conversation. I would have liked to pick his brain on liturgical matters, but felt that he would probably bite my head off. Instead, I asked him at which university he taught.

'If you don't know a basic thing like that, I don't know why you invited me,' he said and carried on eating. I decided to leave it at that.

Eventually we moved across to the hall. Since we were a little late in arriving, the majority of the audience had already taken their seats, and I was pleased to see they had come in numbers. As we approached the platform an enormous man in clerical black came up to Tomkinson and slapped him on the back. The latter seemed to take this remarkably well and I realised I was in the presence of the Beast of Chedderford.

'Petroc,' he boomed, 'how are you?'

In appearance, Father Dermot Byrne, as I preferred to think of him, looked like a combination of prop forward and Boris Karloff. His very size was alarming, as was his physical vitality. I was very glad indeed that he would be on our side in the debate and equally happy that he had so far not deemed it necessary to slap me on the back as well. He spoke with a slight Irish brogue and now repeated the comment he had made earlier on the phone about making mincemeat of the opposition. I looked around to see if Terry Molloy had turned up, and was amazed to see him coming through the doorway wearing a clerical suit every bit as black as Byrne's. He also seemed to have had his hair cut and all in all looked decidedly respectable. Furthermore, he was pushing a wheelchair containing Canon Taylor.

'I couldn't miss this,' said the canon. 'I don't feel very well, Father Page, but I must support you in you hour of need.'

Terry put him in the front row, where the two Bullers, Miranda Phillips and Sloane had all now seated themselves. Nervously, I called for silence and introduced the speaker. This was difficult as I still didn't know anything about him, but I muttered something about him being the most distinguished liturgist working in England today. Tomkinson evidently took this very well, for I saw him assume a self-satisfied expression, but I noticed Bernie Buller looking slightly less happy at my rating of his rival.

I need not have worried about the speech. Where before he had been a tetchy, irritating guest, Tomkinson now became a powerful weapon on the side of the Light. He spoke cogently and coherently in a style that anybody in the audience could have understood, demolishing one by one the shibboleths of the modern liturgical movement. He seemed to have read everything, from ancient sources in a multitude of antique tongues to the latest pronouncements by advanced beardies in California. He even revealed a knowledge of the various pernicious works that had come from Buller's pen and, to my mind at least, demolished the latter's carefully worked-

114

up arguments against the eastwards orientation for the Mass. Buller tried to intervene at one point, but Tomkinson slapped him down pretty quickly and there was no more trouble after that. Where Canon Taylor had come across as a gifted amateur, Tomkinson was undoubtedly the professional down to his fingertips and it dawned on me that we were very lucky to have him. When he finished there was a kind of awed silence in the room and I wondered whether the opposition would have the nerve to take him on.

Eventually, a hand went up.

'Yes, Monsignor Sloane?'

I should have known that my minder would have no qualms about making a fool of himself. Sloane now began his usual guff about a new dawn in the Church and the need for us all to move on to new models of 'Church', but naturally Tomkinson wasn't having any of it. He interrupted Sloane in full flow and told him that all that was just so much nonsense invented by people with no understanding of the organic way in which liturgy had developed over the centuries, and how the current liturgical establishment would not be satisfied until it had destroyed any vestige of the tradition that had come down to us. He proceeded to quote an array of papal pronouncements to show how Sloane's views had been condemned by Pontiff after Pontiff, while Sloane wriggled in his chair and listened reluctantly. It was obvious, of course, that he wasn't convinced, but to have his views dissected so publicly, and in front of people who were, for the moment at least, his parishioners, could not have been pleasant for him.

I decided to intervene myself and ask Tomkinson whether he was in favour of baptismal pools and total immersion. I knew what the answer to this would be, but I wanted the parishioners to hear him say it. He answered that this was yet another progressive fad, encouraged by certain new movements in the Church, and was hardly a necessary practice for parishes today. Drone then stepped in to ask about the old rite of Mass and Tomkinson revealed himself to be a supporter of its wider use, lamenting that the bishops in

England had been so slow to respond to clear papal encouragement of this. And so it went on, Canon Taylor, the Beast and Terry Molloy all chipping into the discussion while the Enemy were forced to sit in the front row looking cross. Phillips made one intervention, adopting her customary bossy tone, but was ignored by Tomkinson, who said quite bluntly that he had already covered the point she was raising and did not propose to go into it again. All in all it was greatly cheering and would, I felt sure, have a big impact on the meeting the following night.

Sloane managed to avoid Tomkinson for the rest of his visit, but when I returned from the station the next morning he seemed back to his usual, chirpy self. I asked him whether he had enjoyed the talk.

'Oh, that old dinosaur doesn't worry me,' he said, smugly. 'Last night was good old knockabout stuff, but tonight we'll see more sober heads prevailing. I'm sure that most of the parishioners here understand that academic questions of that sort bear little relation to the pastoral needs of the Church today.'

Elated by the events of the night before, I felt this was a severe misjudgement of the mood of the meeting and that he would encounter much more opposition than he thought. However, our discussion was now interrupted by the arrival of Spooner.

'What news?' I said, ushering him into the sitting-room.

'Julia's agreed to go out with me,' he replied.

'Really?'

'Yes. I asked her out to dinner and she agreed.'

'Unbelievable.'

I didn't want to discourage him, but was sure that Julia was just trying to be nice. It was imperative that Spooner didn't get the wrong idea and find himself being let down again.

'Now look, Mark,' I said, as the wretched idiot grinned back at me in a paroxysm of happiness. 'Don't get too excited all at once. And whatever you do, don't make any kind of physical move. Just chat politely, drink moderately and listen when she talks about the break-up of her relationship. She probably doesn't want to commit to anyone right now, so don't push it. For once, show some sense.'

'O.K., Father.'

He trotted off, for all the world like a man who'd just won first prize in the lottery. I only hoped Julia knew what she was doing and reflected that she was sometimes too nice for her own good. Returning to Sloane, I asked him why he hadn't told me about the ecumenical service at the Minster. If I thought I was going to embarrass him with this question, I was quite wrong. He took it all in his stride.

'Oh, yes, sorry not to have told you about that. It must have slipped my mind. Do you know, we've actually managed to get the Sisters of Servitude *and* the Nuns of the Paraclete for the service? Quite a coup. That girl who works at the Minster now, Anthea Smith, seems a very good sort. She's asked me to deliver a homily.'

I could see he would enjoy that and was equally sure that the bishop would be all in favour too. I now informed Sloane that I really didn't want to go to the service.

'Oh come on, James,' he protested, trying to sound jocular but unable to hide his annoyance. 'Don't be such a spoilsport. The Churches Together Movement is very important in this area. You and I must show some solidarity here and express our seriousness about the ecumenical cause. You must know how keen the bishop is to get the churches in the diocese working together more closely.'

I knew it all right, but was not keen on the kind of ecumenism that the bishop favoured and suspected that Spencer White felt the same way. It was all right and proper to try to foster good relations with our separated brethren, but not at the expense of watering down our genuine differences. When this was done, the faithful just got confused and began to think that the Catholic Church had abandoned her traditional teachings in favour of an ecumenical mish-mash.

The level of ignorance among people about basic Church teaching was already chronic as a result of courses like *Look At Me, Lord*, and these ecumenical jamborees only made things worse. I would attend the service if ordered to, but not otherwise.

At seven-thirty that evening we were all back in the hall again, but it was immediately clear that the atmosphere this time would be quite different. Sloane was chairing the meeting and I was on the platform with him alongside Miranda Phillips and Lavender Buller, the latter heavily made up and dressed to kill. We had agreed that Sloane would introduce the plan for the reordering, I would then say a few words and Buller would respond. What Phillips was doing up there I wasn't quite sure, but apparently she had some pivotal role on the parish council which made her presence essential.

Sloane now droned on at interminable length about how fortunate we were to be living through a new springtime for the Church and how very soon a new order of harmony and bunny rabbits would prevail. There would be singing and dancing in the streets and life would be one long holiday. He finally got around to talking about the reordering and, to his credit, described it clearly and in some detail. How wonderful it would be, he said, to be able to baptise people by full immersion as had been done in the days of the early Church, a thrilling return to the pure sources of the Gospels. He then began to expatiate on the advantages of the central altar, emphasising the closeness we would all have to the celebrant while sharing the paschal meal. In addition, a spanking new lectionary and chairs would bring us together even more cosily and we would hear the word of the Lord with ever greater clarity. Truly, it would be a time of marvels and wonder.

Eventually Sloane sat down and it was my turn. I had decided to make my opposition to the plan as clear as could be, opposing it on both theological and practical grounds. I reminded the audience of what many of them had heard the previous evening and emphasised that there was absolutely no need to turn their church upside down like this. The arrangement they had at the moment was clearly the traditional one, an arrangement sanctioned by two millennia of history and not the invention of yesterday like the one proposed. Furthermore, this reordering was going to cost money, and lots of it. I reminded them that I had been an accountant before I became a priest and understood very well the financial side of the thing. The parish would be plunged into debt for years to come, all to pay for a fad dreamed up by my predecessor and his acolytes. I didn't mince my words here, leading to a few sharp intakes of breath around the room, especially from Buller and Phillips, one of whom hissed the word 'scandalous.' I emphasised that, although we were very fortunate to have the assistance of Monsignor Sloane at present, I was the parish priest and would have to live with any changes that were made. I could see no reason for the reordering and would therefore be unhappy using the facilities proposed.

In all this, I was able to use as a visual aid a large plan of the new scheme displayed by Sloane to one side of the platform. I pointed out that the chairs suggested for the post-reordering era had no kneelers, though stopped short of saying that I suspected this was a modernist plot to suppress the practice. As I spoke, I tried to gauge what impression I was making but found it extremely difficult to tell. The audience seemed attentive, but I was conscious of as yet knowing few of them well and wondered whether such pleading from me would have much effect against the established figure of Buller. As expected, she spoke well when it was her turn, if a trifle loftily. She placed great stress on the fact that my predecessor had very much wanted this plan and that the whole thing had been agreed by the parish council under his leadership. Who was I, a newcomer and an inexperienced one at that, to come along and dictate to the parish how it should run its affairs? Perhaps in time I would learn how things were done here and would understand why the Catholics of Cheeseminster did not want a return to the dark days of the pre-conciliar era. It was all good stuff, and when the debate was thrown open I noticed how well she had stuffed the audience with her supporters. Sloane helped in this, calling on Tonks and O'Grady to speak next, followed by Phillips and a few others of their kind. Before people like Drone and Julia had a chance to get a word in, the mood of the discussion had already been established in favour of the scheme.

I had asked Sloane in advance whether any vote would be taken on the reordering at the meeting, knowing that such a move would have no actual validity but worried that he could use it against me afterwards. He had been very vague on this point, muttering something about 'seeing how the meeting was going.' At about nine o'clock, he did in fact propose a vote, at which point I immediately intervened and made my objection clear. Sloane now instigated a show of hands to see what the meeting thought of such a move, and there was a narrow majority in favour of proceeding. When the vote came the result was about two to one in favour of the reordering, at which point some women at the back unfurled a WAR! banner and emitted a loud cheer.

I had anticipated this outcome before the meeting and had wondered whether, should such a thing occur, I ought to announce my resignation as parish priest there and then. In the end, for all my strong feelings on the issue, I decided it was too early to do anything quite so drastic as that, but for the moment I was a defeated man, unable to face either the parishioners or Sloane and his many allies. As the meeting broke up, with much hugging and backslapping among the Phillips faction, I left by a side door and stepped out into the night.

(THIRTEEN)

I walked for a long time, traversing the back-streets and suburbs of the town until I found myself in the vicinity of Terry Molloy's parish. The night was cold, for we were now into November, and I began to feel the lack of a coat. There was nothing for it but to knock on Terry's door and demand a whisky. I was greeted by the man himself, holding a bottle of the very same.

'Old Fetterfiddich,' he said. 'Very good.'

I entered and for a while we watched a documentary on television. It was evidently about the proposed repression by the European Union of certain rare dog breeds, but I didn't really take it in. I sipped my whisky, and when the programme had finished poured out my troubles to Terry.

'Do you feel like resigning?' he asked, having heard me out.

'Yes,' I admitted.

'Well, don't.'

He sounded very decided.

'Why not?' I said. 'I'm fed up.'

'That's no reason to go around resigning. You've put up a good fight. Where would leaving get you? You'd only find yourself worse off. Stick around and see what else you can do.'

'But I feel so humiliated.'

'That'll wear off. This isn't the end yet, you know. Now, I think it's about time we had another whisky. There's some eighteen year old Mucklecarrick down here somewhere.'

He groped around on the floor near the sofa and eventually found the bottle he was looking for. I accepted another glass and asked him whether I should continue to fight the reordering scheme or give in gracefully.

'That's a difficult one,' he replied, obviously giving the matter some serious thought. 'The trouble is, your benighted predecessor and his cronies have so firmly implanted the idea in people's heads that a momentum has been built up. Now that Sloane has publicly given his backing to the scheme you'd be seen to be in open revolt against the bishop if you carried on fighting it. You're obviously absolutely right to be opposed to something which is ridiculous and a waste of money, but after today you probably wouldn't survive much longer in the parish if you kept up your opposition. The WAR! ladies would cause such a stink in the press that the bishop would have to get rid of you. Remember, this is a campaign of attrition. We can't expect to win it all at once. Any gains at all should be considered as victories. Once Sloane has gone, you'll be able to push things on a bit in other areas.'

I wasn't sure about this. The modernists had already shown pretty clearly that you could only provoke them so far before they came in and stamped all over you. After all, that was precisely why Sloane had been brought in in the first place. However, after about the fourth whisky I was beginning to feel defiant again and ready to regroup my forces for another go. As Terry now pointed out, it was not as if I was entirely without allies in the parish and, given time, these could be augmented. I staggered out into the street feeling much more hopeful than before.

The following morning I surprised Sloane over breakfast with an unexpected cheeriness, his amazement being increased when I told him that in the light of the meeting I would withdraw my opposition to the plan. As far as I was concerned, I said, the reordering could go ahead and the builders move in. He seemed absolutely delighted by this and announced that he would be leaving Cheeseminster just as soon as the Parish Council had met and approved precisely that. This, apparently, would be after the ecumenical service but before Christmas.

The next few weeks were a period of welcome calm. The first thing to do was to cut short the series of talks on the liturgy and I informed Terry that his help would no longer be needed. After Tomkinson's effort, I felt, nothing further could really be said. Meanwhile, I continued to say the old rite Mass in private on days when Sloane was saying the public Mass and went about my normal pastoral work in a mood of resignation. The second Sunday Mass for the CRC went as well as the first, and I was gratified to see that Miller did indeed turn up, though the barking of his dog outside the church drew some complaints from the more established members of the congregation. Furthermore, Mrs. Moss announced that her choir would be able to sing at the following month's Mass, so here at least was one area of my life where all was well and I was still master of my destiny. In fact, I was impressed by the general attitude of the CRC members, who remained terribly grateful to me for what I was doing and sympathised with me over the reordering. Some of them had been at the parish meeting and had been appalled by the conduct of the debate, so here, I felt, were more allies who could be added to the cause. It was clear that by agreeing to say the old rite Mass I had created for myself a ready-made body of support that might prove extremely useful later on.

The only other interesting thing going on was Spooner's friendship with Julia, which seemed to go from strength to strength. He continued to adore her without pouncing on her and she, as far as I could work out, enjoyed being with someone who was so obviously in need of help. In the aftermath of her break-up with Ray, she seemed to need someone on whom to lavish her altruistic instincts and I, for one, was delighted about this since it took the pressure off me. So long as it didn't go any further than that, all would be fine, but I now knew Spooner well enough to wonder how long this happy state of affairs could continue. I met them outside the Minster as I headed towards the Churches Together service, which I had agreed to attend on the condition that I didn't have to take part. It was a bitterly cold Sunday afternoon late in the month and Julia was wearing a coat, hat and gloves. Spooner, however, had none of these accoutrements and looked as if he might soon freeze to death. His face was white and his hair appeared frozen to his head.

'What are you two doing here?' I asked, troubled that they felt it necessary to attend such a dubious occasion. Spooner explained that he was planning to write a hostile article about the service, which he would send to *Get Real*, the magazine of the CRC. Julia's reply was equally reassuring.

'One of the nuns is another of my aunts,' she said. 'I wouldn't hear the end of it if I didn't make an appearance.'

We went in and took a seat towards the back. Spooner immediately pulled out a notebook and began to write furiously, even though nothing was actually happening. Soon the Minster was full, a three-line whip clearly having been imposed on their people by all the clergymen in the Cheeseminster area. I noticed the Methodist minister sailing down the aisle in some sort of get-up peculiar to his communion, together with his opposite number at the United Reformed Church, the pair of them having called on Sloane during the week to make his acquaintance and arrange aspects of the service. Meanwhile, Anthea Smith was very much in evidence, her hair freshly trimmed and burnished and dog-collar firmly in place. She was obviously in some sort of flap about the reserved seating, for every now and again she emerged from a kind of ante-room and engaged herself in animated conversation with a robed functionary at the front of the nave. After a while, however, a hush descended, broken only by the tranquil playing of the organ, and I wondered what fireworks awaited us.

They were not long in coming. Suddenly there was a blare of trumpets from the choir loft and a procession emerged from a side aisle. Some weird organ music accompanied this, like the opening of a horror film, and the massed corps of nuns swung into view. The Sisters of Servitude were at the front, all six of them, dressed in long, rainbow-coloured robes and swinging their arms from side to side like creatures from a nightmare. As they did so, they lurched occasionally towards the ground or flung their arms up high, the movements being not very well synchronised owing to the infirmity of the participants. The Nuns of the Paraclete were a much more agile lot, some of them perhaps as young as forty, and they hurried on behind, skipping occasionally to the music and letting out periodic shouts of ecstasy. Soon the music reached an almost unbearable volume, with the trumpets blaring and the organ still pounding away, only to give way suddenly to the tune of the opening hymn.

> *We are children of one Father, let's be one!*
> *Oh, we all love one another, let's be one!*
> *We are children of the Lord,*
> *And one Church must be secured,*
> *Oh, we all love one another,*
> *Let's be one!*

This went on and on as the procession wound its way interminably round the church. After heading down the main aisle, it snaked its way up one side and down another, finally arriving at the sanctuary with a further blast of trumpets and a roll of drums. Sloane was lurking somewhere towards the back, looking massively smug and beaming at people he knew as he passed them, while Spencer White traipsed along looking as if he would rather be anywhere else but here. Anthea Smith was the most enthusiastic participant among the clergy, singing with gusto, her big teeth flashing under the Minster's lights as she clapped her way down the various aisles. It was she who introduced the service from the lectern when all movement had finally stopped.

'What joy,' she said, in her curious, lisping voice. 'What joy to come together to sing, to pray, to dance. What joy to put aside our differences and join in common worship, to praise the Lord with one voice and proclaim our love. I welcome you in the name of that love and trust that today the bonds that bind us may bring us ever closer.'

125

As she said this, she spread her arms wide and smiled rapturously, injecting a note of delirium into her voice that made the whole performance curiously distasteful. For her, life clearly held nothing more thrilling than an ecumenical service and I could only pity the poor woman.

We now had a couple of readings, inevitably given by children, followed by another ghastly hymn. It was only then that I noticed Tonks lurking at the side of the sanctuary with a group of his regulars, and a glance at the service sheet told me that we were about to be treated to an extract from his *People's Mass*. Not only that, but the nuns were about to spring into action again. This time they broadened their repertoire with the use of diaphanous scarves, swirling them this way and that as they cavorted across a platform in front of the altar. Just as they were about to execute a particularly difficult *paso doble*, the most ancient of them all suddenly had a seizure and was seen limping off as the others gamely carried on. I noticed Spooner furiously taking extra notes at this point, before leaving his seat and heading down the aisle to take a photograph of the remaining Sisters in action. Tonks was soon encouraging the congregation to clap along, and the whole thing degenerated into such farce that I had to step outside and take a quick breather. Here I found Terry Molloy smoking a cigarette.

'Isn't it dreadful?' I said.

'It's going to get worse,' he replied. 'We haven't had Sloane yet.'

Entering again, we were just in time to see the man himself approaching the lectern, accompanied by Anthea Smith, who announced that she was going to interview him.

'Welcome, Monsignor Sloane, to our gathering,' she said.

'Call me Rory,' he replied.

Smith nearly had palpitations at this point, but pulled herself together enough to ask Sloane what he felt the chances were for reunion between the Churches in the near future.

'Quite good, I think,' said Sloane. 'What we need is a unity of love. There may be differences about things such as intercommunion and women priests, but if we all progress together at the local level then a great deal can be achieved. 'Never do apart what can be done together' seems to me to be an excellent slogan for the Churches in Cheeseminster and one that I am sure we will all strive to follow. Very soon I will no longer be among you, but I am certain that the momentum I can feel today in this Minster will be unstoppable. Do not let yourselves be cowed by those who would put obstacles in the way of unity, but seek always to act through charity to achieve our common goals. May God bless you, Anthea, and all you are trying to do.'

This was almost too much for his interviewer, who emitted a prolonged and rather curious giggling noise and nearly dropped the microphone. She now moved away to recover from all the excitement and Sloane was allowed to pontificate alone about the various initiatives that were currently being pursued on the ecumenical front. It seemed that inter-Church study groups were the next thing on the agenda.

'Parishioners of the various Churches will meet together in small gatherings to discuss what unites and what, sadly, still divides us. Through this we will come to understand each other more and realise that only through sharing can we build up the Church of Christ in the Gorgehampton area. The Roman Catholic diocese here is fully committed to this process and will take a leading part in the setting-up of these groups. Where once, perhaps, we were a little backward in ecumenism, we now intend to be leaders. There can be no going back on this important mission for the Church.'

Needless to say, he was interrupted frequently by fervent applause and the speech threatened to go on for several hours. Finally, however, it drew to a close and I felt it was now safe to make my exit, confident that I knew what Buller and Phillips would be up to in the near future. The modernist bandwagon was clearly rolling again and I resolved to do whatever I could to counter this latest manifestation.

FOURTEEN

Not long afterwards, Sloane took his leave. The Parish Council had met and, as promised, I had made no further objections to the reordering. From now on, Masses would have to take place in the parish hall, for once the builders had moved in it would be impossible to try to conduct services in the church. To give him his due, O'Grady was very helpful with this, even consenting to help me set up the altar rails at the front of the makeshift sanctuary. I think he was secretly pleased that the only altar that could be used in the hall was the portable one he had made for Sloane, though how he would accommodate his full team of lads and girlies was clearly going to be a problem. There was no room for manoeuvre at all and I did not welcome the idea of about twenty children invading such a confined space.

'I think we'll have to have a rota, Jim,' he said, as we moved some of the outlandish servers' costumes across to the hall. 'Some of them will be terribly upset, but they'll have to live with it. I've already explained about the reordering and how they'll have to get used to a new system again when we get back into the church. Some of the little ones cried – it was tragic.'

Tonks was equally exercised as to how he was going to get the full complement of his choir into the tiny space. Every day during the move I saw him pacing the area and trying to decide exactly where they were all going to put themselves. Buller and Phillips made occasional visits to check that I was doing nothing untoward, the latter objecting that I had brought the kneelers in with the chairs.

'There's no need for those,' she said. 'We can stand instead. There's so little room in here that it would be foolish to waste it by using the kneelers. Have you learned nothing, James?'

I told her that the kneelers were staying and made sure that O'Grady did not have a key to the hall as he had at the church. There would be no fiddling around with the arrangements here.

The question now arose as to how exactly to conduct the various Masses in the absence of Sloane. During the week I had become thoroughly habituated to using the old rite privately on the days when he was performing, and would have very much liked to have gone public with it. This, however, would have required the bishop's permission, one that I knew would not be forthcoming. The more I examined the differences between the old rite and the new, the more the former continued to impress me, and even celebrating the latter in Latin was becoming disagreeable. The idea of having to go back to saying it in English was almost intolerable, but I decided that, for the interim at least, it would be better to do so, at least on the days formerly covered by Sloane. Latin Masses in the new rite could continue on the other days, especially now that everyone was used to this and seemed to approve of it. Before he had left, Sloane had extracted a promise from me that I would leave the Sunday Masses alone, at least until the new year. He said that the parishioners had no need of further upheavals, especially with the additional move from the church into the hall. I was tempted to remark that none of these changes had been wished by me, but, fearing that he might not leave at all if I refused to comply, agreed. I therefore faced once more the kind of eleven o'clock Mass that had greeted me when I first arrived, a nightmare that would test my resolve to the limit.

The morning after Sloane's departure, a bright Saturday in early December, I settled down to a cooked breakfast feeling that, despite the horrors to come the next day, nothing could spoil the sheer joy of not having His Oiliness breathing down my neck. I was soon snapped out of this reverie, however, by the ringing of the front doorbell and the arrival of Julia. It was obvious that she was in some distress.

'Father, I must speak to you,' she said, looking more dishevelled than I had ever seen her and bursting into the house at some speed. I asked her what the matter was.

'It's Mark,' she said. 'He's gone mad.'

In due course she calmed down enough to be able to tell me what had happened. It seemed that the previous night she had driven Spooner over to Gorgehampton to what was generally regarded as the best restaurant in the county. The idea had been Spooner's and he had said in advance that he would pay for their meals. This had rather alarmed Julia, knowing that he existed entirely on his student grant, and she had only reluctantly agreed. Furthermore, she was becoming rather tired of hearing his tales of woe about women and, although he had never made any physical advances towards her, she was not naïve enough to think he wasn't interested. When she picked him up from his student hovel in Cheeseminster she was amazed to see him wearing a dinner jacket and jaunty bow tie, an outfit wholly at odds with his usual scruffiness and one never before seen. He appeared somewhat tenser than usual and had put some kind of oil on his rather wispy hair, slicking it down so that he looked like a fugitive from the Jazz Age. He was also wearing an overpowering aftershave that led her, despite the coolness of the night, to wind the car window down so as to be able to breath some fresh air. All in all, it had not been a propitious start to the evening.

No sooner had they arrived at the restaurant and started their meal than Spooner made an unexpected move, suddenly falling to the ground on one knee and offering her a ring he had kept concealed in a box in the top pocket of his jacket. Apparently, this was a proposal of marriage, which he accompanied by a speech expressing his undying devotion to Julia and praising in no uncertain terms her extraordinary beauty and loveliness. She was so shocked by this that she knocked over a glass of white wine, which spilled over Spooner's head. Nothing daunted, he had got up again and waited for her reply. This, when it came, had distressed him so

131

much that he was unable to eat another bite of what had promised to be an excellent dinner. In fact, he stopped speaking altogether and simply sat in his chair staring into space as if to go on living was no longer an option. Realising that they had better get away before a scene developed, Julia had called for the bill and then practically dragged the helpless sap from his chair and out of the building.

On their arrival at Spooner's flat, he had refused to get out of the car and she had asked him whether he wanted to come over to her place and have a drink to help him calm down.

'Was that really wise?' I said, worried now as to where this account was taking us.

'I couldn't leave the poor lunatic alone in that state,' she replied. 'I was afraid he'd do something stupid.'

'And did he?' I asked.

'Oh, yes. I'm coming to that.'

Spooner had accepted a whisky and sat in an armchair sipping at it, his shoulders hunched and his face tearstained. Julia tried then to explain that she was greatly flattered by his proposal but that he would have to accept that she was not the woman for him. After a while he had calmed down a bit and they had begun to talk of more general matters, the evening taking a much more positive turn and Spooner even managing to seem quite recovered. He had accepted another whisky, but it soon became clear to Julia that he was in fact dead drunk, having knocked a fair bit back even before she had picked him up. Before she knew it, he had dozed off where he was sitting and nothing she could do would wake him up. She had thought about calling a taxi, but in the end decided to leave him there and go to bed. This proved her second mistake.

At some time in the middle of the night, and what she later discovered was three a.m., she was woken by the sound of someone entering her bedroom. Turning on the light, she saw Spooner advancing towards her, dressed only in his underpants and moaning 'Julia, I love you' in a kind of deranged frenzy. It was clear he meant to get into her bed.

'What did you do?' I asked, agog.

'I threw my alarm clock at him.'

I was impressed.

'Did that do the trick?'

'Well, it certainly surprised him. He was still completely drunk. Then the alarm kept ringing and I shouted at him that I was calling the police. At this point he ran out of the room.'

'Did you follow him?'

'Not for a bit, no. I was too stunned. When I did get up I found he'd left the flat.'

'Clothed or unclothed?'

'Clothed, thank God. Then I rang his mobile, but there was no reply. Now I don't know what to do.'

I pondered what the best solution would be. Having made Julia a cup of coffee, I tried ringing Spooner but there was no reply. I felt that it was critical I reached him before he did something very stupid indeed. If I read his psychology right, he would feel enormous remorse once he had sobered up a bit and the sense of guilt would be overwhelming. Normally when he had behaved badly he came to me for confession, and the fact that he hadn't rushed round that very morning was cause for alarm in itself. I tried to think where he might have gone. Were Julia and I his only confidants? I had never seen him talking to anyone else, but this did not mean that there wasn't somebody at the university to whom he was in the habit of pouring out his troubles. Fortunately, as I was trying to calm Julia down again, she too being wracked by feelings of guilt about what had happened, the telephone rang and I heard Terry Molloy's voice on the other end of the line.

'Jim, do you know someone called Mark Spooner?' he said. 'I've got him here with me at the moment.'

'Thank goodness for that. How is he?'

'Not very well. Come and see for yourself.'

Counselling Julia that it might be better if she went home, I drove up to Molloy's house to find Spooner perched on a chair in the kitchen and looking as if he and Death were wondering whether an imminent encounter might not be a good thing. His hair was covered with a kind of slime and his clothes were absolutely filthy. When Terry and I came in, he did not look up.

'Mark,' I said. 'Where have you been?'

He did not reply, merely groaning a little and rocking backwards and forwards. Terry now made him a cup of tea, while I tried to coax from Spooner his version of events. Eventually he became more coherent.

'I've done some terrible things, Father,' he said. 'I don't think she'll ever forgive me.'

'Tell me about it.'

'No. I couldn't.'

'Do you want me to hear your confession?'

'Yes.'

When this was over, he revived quite considerably and I was able to give him some much needed advice.

'Go and have a bath,' I said. 'When you've recovered a bit and changed your clothes, come over to the presbytery at St. Aelred's and we'll have a chat. Why are you so dirty, by the way?'

'I fell into a ditch.'

'Ah.'

Later that morning, he duly appeared and spent a good half an hour pouring out to me his love for Julia, explaining how life without her would be a pointless, hollow sham, devoid of meaning. I told him I thought he was being unduly pessimistic. He disagreed, and we went on like this for some time until he eventually said, 'you don't understand.'

'But I do,' I said, frustrated now by his stubbornness. 'I told you before, I've had a great deal of experience of affairs of the heart. You always feel like this at the beginning, but somehow or other life always moves on and you meet someone else.'

'I don't want to meet someone else.'

'Not now, maybe, but some time in the future you will.'

'I won't.'

'Of course you will. Look, if I were you, I wouldn't attempt to see Julia for a while. Believe me, it would be pointless pursuing her and you'd be much better off forgetting all about her.'

He shook his head.

'That's impossible. I think about her all the time. She's the most beautiful woman in the world.'

'That may be so, but it doesn't mean she wants to marry you.'

'Did she say that?'

'Yes, she did. And anyway, she told you so herself. By the way, I hope the ring you bought wasn't too expensive.'

'Oh, but it was. I had to take out a loan.'

'Oh, no!'

'I'm not taking it back, though. One day she'll want it.'

'Don't be a fool.'

'I'm not. Sooner or later she'll see I'm perfect for her.'

It was hopeless. Eventually he sloped off, looking as forlorn as I had ever seen him, and I wondered how long it would take him to recover from the events of the night before. I just hoped he wouldn't pester Julia, a very live possibility given his obsessive temperament. Further problems from Spooner were all I needed now and I prayed fervently that he would manage to keep his head.

(FIFTEEN)

The following day, the first Sunday in Advent, I met Julia after the eight o'clock Mass and she told me that Spooner had not rung her up or attempted to see her. This was a relief and I prayed that things would stay like that. Normally, he would have been at this Mass but, following my advice, had evidently decided to stay away. As I returned to the hall to prepare for the eleven o'clock he duly appeared, looking as if all the stuffing had been knocked out of him but otherwise all right, and I commended him for not having tried to contact Julia. This seemed to cheer him a little.

'Yes,' he said. 'I'm being strong. I have entered a world of pain, but I can cope.'

There was a fanatical gleam in his eyes as he said this, but I thought on the whole this was better than other moods I might have expected. No sooner had he entered the hall than Miranda Phillips appeared.

'Good morning, James,' she said. 'Have the builders moved in yet?'

'They're coming tomorrow.'

She assumed an expression of quiet satisfaction.

'I do wish you could see how wonderful this reordering is for the church, James. Why not spend some time at the Pastoral Centre after Christmas and talk to Bernie? He'll show you how important it is.'

'No thanks, Miranda. I'm spending a week at Notre Dame-de-Monts.'

She reacted as if I had emitted a noxious smell. This was a plan I had formed only a few days before, while surfing the net to see if I could find a retreat house where they said the old rite of Mass on a daily basis. The Abbaye de Notre Dame-de-Monts was in the Languedoc region of the south of France and housed some fifty young monks who were all devoted to

136

the traditional Latin Mass. The establishment had been approved by the Pope in the nineteen-eighties and was now a flourishing concern, with vocations pouring in from all sides. I thought that a few days there after Christmas might help restore my sanity and give me a chance to work out my plan for the future.

Deciding it was better to change the subject, I asked Phillips about the hot topic of the moment.

'When are you having your first meeting of the ecumenical discussion group, Miranda?'

She brightened again at this, clearly surprised that I should be interested. Nothing in her expression suggested she had guessed the real reason for my curiosity.

'Next Thursday night. We're meeting at my house in Poulton Lacey. Given your views on just about everything, I imagined you wouldn't want to come.'

'On the contrary, I wouldn't miss it for the world. When should I turn up?'

She gave me a time and then, still looking a little bemused, disappeared into the hall. I followed her, heading for the kitchen that was now serving as a sacristy, and found a scene out of an Hieronymus Bosch vision of Hell. The place was a seething mass of tiny children with O'Grady somewhere in the middle issuing orders in a strained voice. The noise and the smell were appalling.

'Get these children out of here, Desmond,' I shouted above the hubbub. 'I've got to get ready for Mass.'

Eventually, he cleared the room, and when I had finally vested and mentally prepared myself for the ordeal to come I resurfaced and told him that we would process around the outside of the building and enter through the front door. Even this proved problematic. The procession turned out to be far too wide for the narrow aisle left by the hastily arranged chairs, and by the time we reached the sanctuary the whole thing had developed into a rugby scrum. When we tried to genuflect together, some of the children fell over each other in a heap. Tonks, meanwhile, was conducting the congregation with gusto in a rendition of *He Is Lord, The Lord Is Love* and had placed his choir in such a way as to shut off the left side of the sanctuary. To say that the Mass that ensued was a shambles would be a considerable understatement. I tried to reason with O'Grady afterwards.

'You've got to get rid of some of these altar servers,' I said. 'It just isn't working.'

'I take your point, Jim.'

'I could barely move around the altar. It isn't surprising that one boy fainted.'

'You're right, Jim, you're right.'

'Can you please get that rota organised?'

'Don't worry. By next week it'll all be sorted.'

I wasn't convinced. In fact, I was beginning to wonder whether it might not be a good idea to provoke another row with the man and hope that he would stage a fresh walkout. On the other hand, having to rely on Spooner's services again might well drive me over the edge. It seemed all my troubles were beginning again and if I'd thought that Sloane's departure would bring me any real relief, I was rapidly learning I was wrong.

The following Tuesday, I had arranged with Julia to go over to the school and hear the children's confessions. I could imagine what Sloane would have thought of this. He was a fervent believer in general absolution, that is, getting everyone together on an evening before Christmas and absolving the lot of them in a group. This, of course, was banned by the Vatican, so to provide a fig leaf Sloane was busily going round the diocesan clergy trying to persuade them to help him out. His idea was to have five or six priests in the sanctuary at the cathedral who would encourage the congregation to come forward and confess a sin or two to make it legitimate. There would also probably be some modernist babble about 'confessing one good thing you've done well, too' to counterbalance any supposed negativity about the sacrament. I learned all this from Terry Molloy, who had delighted in telling Sloane that he was busy that evening, even though in fact he would be watching television as usual. I, of course, was not approached.

I met Julia in the staff room and asked her if Spooner was sticking to his policy of self-restraint.

'Well, yes and no,' she said, looking less than happy. 'He hasn't rung me or called, but last night I was closing my curtains and saw him standing outside in the street. When I looked again about half an hour later he was still there.'

I made a mental note to talk to him again and we moved off to Julia's classroom. Before taking the children across to the hall for confessions, I decided it might be better to prepare them a little. I knew that very few of them ever frequented the sacrament and, remembering my previous discussion with them on the subject, wanted to make sure that they actually knew what a sin was. The occasional children I had had in the past had been very hazy about it.

'Now then,' I said. 'It's important before going into confession to make an examination of conscience. Can anyone tell me what that is?'

Blank stares greeted this question, so I explained briefly that they must recall to mind all the sins they had committed since their last visit.

'What if you can't remember?' I was now asked by the deranged-looking boy who had been one of my interlocutors before.

'Well, just do your best,' I replied. 'But you must confess all serious sins, so it's terribly important to try to remember them.'

This got them thinking a bit, and a girl with spots now asked me to name a few. At this point I asked Julia to distribute some leaflets about confession that I had brought with me and highlighted some of the more serious sins on the list. Some of the children began to look extremely chastened.

'Bloody hell,' said one.

'I didn't know any of this stuff,' said another, clearly shocked by what she was reading. 'What's tax evasion?'

I told her she could rest easy in her mind about that one. Then there was a query about contraceptives, accompanied by a lot of giggling, and I explained that not only was sex before marriage wrong, but also the use of artificial methods of birth control.

'Can't you do *anything*, then?' asked a ginger-haired boy.

'Of course you can,' I replied. 'You just can't do bad things.'

'But I like bad things,' said the boy.

'Well, you shouldn't. Before you go into confession, pray for a real conversion of life.'

'All right.'

We went through a few other sins, perhaps more relevant to what they might actually have been getting up to, and then moved across to the hall. In the end, things went quite well, and after it was all over I told them that now they had made a good start to confessing properly they should try to continue.

Emboldened by the success of this venture, I drove out to Poulton Lacey on Thursday evening in a more cheerful frame of mind. The village was one of the most attractive in the area and house prices were reputed to be high. Phillips lived in an enormous villa on the outskirts, sheltered from the road by trees and a long, gravel drive, and she explained when I arrived that she had inherited the house from her father, with whom she had lived before he died of cancer a few years before. I was the first to arrive, so there were an awkward few minutes before the other members of the group turned up. In due course we were joined by Anthea Smith, who seemed to know Phillips very well, Tonks, who had brought his guitar, and, much to my delight, Mavis Bird. The latter was now definitely a fan of mine and in a quiet moment expressed the hope that Phillips, whom she regarded as a 'bossy woman', would not dominate proceedings too much. Finally, two elderly Anglican ladies arrived and we were ready to start.

'I thought we'd begin with a prayer,' said Phillips.

At this point it would have been customary to ask the priest present to lead the prayer, but Phillips wasn't having any of that. She obviously intended to say it herself. Then she remarked that it would be a very good idea if we burst into song, so Tonks began to strum away on his guitar and we staggered through a few verses of the wretched hymn that had kicked off the ecumenical service. Finally, Phillips opened the discussion, whining on at some length about how awful it was that Christians were divided and how much better things would be if we were One. There was much enthusiastic agreement at this, especially from Anthea Smith, who had tried to start some clapping during the hymn but had stopped when no-one else joined in. After Smith's contribution, one of the Anglican ladies asked why Catholics didn't allow Anglicans to receive communion in their churches. I was about to answer this, when Phillips said:

'Yes, it's a very, very sad state of affairs, isn't it? Sharing at the table of the Lord's banquet is so important for us all and I feel that my own Church has shown a great lack of love in refusing the sacraments to our fellow Christians.'

I tried to butt in at this point and explain that there were very good reasons for the Catholic ban, but Phillips waved at me to shut up and instead invited the Anglican lady to agree with her that the Catholic Church was indeed very, very wicked in this area. Then Tonks piped up and began to complain about the 'conservatism', as he called it, of the current Pope and how he was hoping that the Holy Father would get a move on and die so that the new age of modernism could finally proceed unchecked. I finally managed to get a word in now and told him that I thought his hopes were vain and that the wishy-washy Church he was looking for would never arrive. He begged to differ, at which point Mavis Bird piped up and agreed with me, much to the obvious disapproval of Phillips. The discussion then turned into a free for all, the general gist from everyone but me and Miss Bird being that union between the Churches would only be achieved when the Catholic Church had agreed to ordain

141

women, allow its priests to marry and had got rid of all the silly teaching about contraception. I felt I had walked into a sixties time-warp and vigorously tried to defend Catholic teaching in the areas attacked. However, it was clear that Phillips and co. had made their minds up and had no intention of listening to reactionary opinions like mine. As I had feared, the group was simply developing into a vehicle for sowing dissent, creating false expectations amongst our separated brethren that the Catholic Church was about to alter its teaching to fit in with Protestants. When I voiced this opinion, I thought Phillips was going to order me from the house, but she satisfied herself, Tony Blair-like, with a withering attack on the 'forces of conservatism' and people like me who wanted us all to return to the dark ages. I had heard all this before, of course, but was satisfied that the Anglicans would at least go home realising that there was more than one point of view in the Catholic Church.

On my drive back to Cheeseminster I decided to head down to the road where Julia lived and see if Spooner had elected to stage another vigil outside her flat. I found him pacing backwards and forwards under a street lamp, holding a bunch of flowers.

'Get in the car,' I said.

'I don't want to, Father.'

'Get in the car!'

He refused to budge.

'You can't make me,' he whined. 'I want to talk to Julia and explain why I did what I did.'

'Now isn't the time.'

Eventually, after talking to him for about half an hour, I persuaded him that springing himself on Julia so soon after the 'unfortunate incident', as we were now calling it, would not be wise. Wearily, he opened the door and settled himself into the seat beside me. The flowers looked decidedly the worse for wear, for the evening had been a wet one and Spooner himself was now soaked to the skin. I drove him back to his flat, an apartment at the top of what seemed to be a condemned building, and he asked me to come in for a coffee. Feeling that it might be a good idea to keep him company for a little longer, I climbed some dingy stairs with him and we entered what must be the filthiest room I have ever seen. That there weren't rats crawling all over the place was a miracle. Half-eaten Chinese takeaways were littered across the chairs and empty cartons of milk were strewn across the floor. Beer cans were everywhere, as were mugs half-filled with cold tea. The only pristine object appeared to be the computer, an ancient model pushed up against one wall on a tatty-looking desk. I noticed that the particularly nasty, nicotine-stained wallpaper was peeling in several places and that the room was lit by a single bulb with no lampshade. Altogether, it was as depressing a bedsit as I had ever seen.

'Can't you afford anything better?' I asked Spooner, as he attempted to clear a space on one of the chairs. 'This place is dreadful.'

'Is it?' he asked, seeming genuinely surprised. 'I quite like it.'

'Do you ever have guests?'

'Not as a rule. I generally visit other people.'

'Did Julia ever come here?'

'No.'

As soon as I had asked the question, I realised it had been a mistake to mention the sacred name, because he now slumped down into a chair covered with old newspapers and stared gloomily into the middle distance. The flowers lay drooping on the floor beside his seat. I decided that what he needed was a plan.

'Let's turn your computer on,' I said. 'You can show me the internet Catholic dating site.'

'All right.'

He didn't sound terribly enthusiastic, but did as I had suggested. It turned out that he had entered his details on the site and I asked if I could read them. They were inscribed next to a picture of him that made him look like an axe-murderer having a bad hair day, and informed me that he liked going to pubs, reading science-fiction and serving at Mass. He apparently wanted someone in her early twenties who also liked pubs and was outgoing, friendly and attractive. It would help if she were slim and preferred the Latin Mass. I asked him if he had had any replies.

'None so far,' he said. 'I'll just check my messages.'

It was evidently his lucky day, for a girl had actually contacted him in response to his entry. He read her details and pronounced himself satisfied with what he had seen.

'I'm not contacting her, though,' he said, firmly.

'Why not?'

'I cannot betray Julia.'

It took me a further half an hour to persuade him that he would have to look on his friendship with Julia as a thing of the past and that he should contact this girl without delay. He finally promised to do so and I took my leave.

'Live in the present,' I said as I left the flat. 'It's good, Catholic doctrine.'

He nodded and I returned to the presbytery, thoroughly worn out by the night's events.

SIXTEEN

With every fibre of my being I was now yearning for my post-Christmas break at the monastery, but I still had to get through the rest of Advent and Christmas itself. The only pleasure that awaited me during this time was the monthly Mass for the CRC. When Hubert Drone heard that I was off to the Notre Dame-de-Monts he commended me on my choice and said that he had visited it himself while holidaying in the south of France.

'You'll love it, Father,' he said. 'Nothing but traditional Masses every day in beautiful surroundings, with excellent food to boot. If I were still single, I'd be off there like a shot.'

It has been said by people whose judgment I respect that my singing voice is quite good, so when Mrs. Moss announced that the Gregorian choir was ready to perform at the next old rite Mass I was perfectly happy to do my bit. Once again, Mr. Miller turned up, this time with his daughter and minus the dog. I asked Leighanne afterwards what she had thought of the Mass.

'A bit weird, isn't it?' she said. 'But I suppose it was all right really. Don't tell dad I said that, though, or he'll make me come again. I only went this time 'cos he said he'd take me down the pub.'

Impressed by Miller's tactics, I wondered whether I could learn from them, but before I had a chance to do any more thinking along these lines I was accosted by Spooner.

'I'm seeing that internet girl,' he muttered, gloomily.

'Good.'

'Don't tell Julia, though.'

'I wouldn't dream of it.'

'I still love her, you know.'

'Of course.'

145

Julia herself had also attended the Mass, but had slipped off pretty quickly afterwards, perhaps fearing Spooner's approach. When I returned to the presbytery I was annoyed to hear the phone ringing and even more irritated when I recognised Tonks' voice at the end of the line. I asked him what he wanted.

'It's about the Christmas party,' he said. 'Can I put up some posters in the hall?'

'Go right ahead.'

'You see, this is going to be a big occasion. That's why we're doing a Nurdles gig at it. All the profits will go to the reordering.'

'How wonderful.'

'I'm glad you think so, Jim.'

I'd forgotten about this event, which was apparently held every year in the parish. Normally it took place in the hall, but this time, because of the presence of the Nurdles and because I had refused to allow the hall to be used, it was going to be staged in the function room of the pub opposite the church. I remembered the last Nurdles 'gig' and wondered whether it could possibly be as eventful as that.

When the evening came round, a Friday just before Christmas, I was not disappointed. Arriving at the pub I found it already thick with smoke, with the Nurdles tuning up for their first session of the evening. The posters had warned me that, as was customary, the occasion would be a fancy dress one, the theme chosen this year being along country and western lines. Furthermore, an additional attraction, billed loudly on the posters, was that the Beast of Chedderford would be performing with Tonks in some of the Nurdles' numbers. Byrne's penchant for this kind of thing had made him very popular with his rustic parishioners and had undoubtedly contributed to the very large crowd who had turned up in the pub that evening. Most had gone along with the theme and were dressed in jeans, check shirts and large hats, O'Grady looking particularly ridiculous in a false Zapata moustache. He offered to buy me a drink.

'No hard feelings, eh, Jim?' he said.

'What do you mean?'

'Well, we didn't exactly get off to a good start, did we? I'm sorry about that now and since it's the season of good will I must buy you a pint.'

The next to approach me at the bar was the Beast himself.

'Howdy, partner,' he said, slapping me on the back and drawing out a toy pistol which he stuck in my ribs. 'The fastest draw in the West Country, that's me. Let me get you one.'

'I've already got a pint.'

'Well, that never stopped me having another one. What's your poison?'

He was in full costume and looked, as I supposed was the idea, like a clerical John Wayne. When he handed me the drink, I asked what he was going to sing.

'Oh, a few Johnny Cash numbers,' he replied. 'I specialise in those. Well, see you, partner.'

He swaggered off, towering over the people he passed, and made his way up to the stage. Pausing only to down his pint, he joined Tonks and the rest of the band and they went into the first number. After two Johnny Cash songs, received with much whooping and applause, he left to a standing ovation and the band settled down to its usual stuff about nurdling gurdlers and chicken wanglers. Tonks was as energetic as ever, but managed to keep himself upright and at the interval was still in one piece. He too now approached me.

'Did you like that, Jim?' he asked.

'I'm warming to it,' I said, trying to be diplomatic.

'Thought you would in the end. I still haven't given you that CD, have I?'

'No.'

'Must remedy that. Come new year you'll be singing all our numbers to yourself in the bath.'

'I wouldn't count on it, Greg.'

By now I had drunk several pints and was in fact beginning to enjoy myself. I reflected that, apart from one or two sessions with Terry Molloy, I had not really let my hair down since arriving in the parish. War-war and jaw-jaw had got in the way of any kind of enjoyment. I liked a good pint as much as the next man, but things had been so difficult that I hadn't had a chance to have any real fun. It struck me that this evening was turning into a good thing. O'Grady had been nice to me, Tonks seemed to have got over his animosity and everyone in the parish was having a good time. I had even noticed the Bullers singing along to one or two of the tunes, Lavender Buller looking suitably ridiculous in a denim skirt and spangly top. As for Phillips, she had turned up in her usual druidic outfit, to which Tonks, irritated by her failure to come in costume, had attached a sheriff's star.

As the band struck up again I maintained my position at the bar, wondering who would come over and talk to me next. It was the Misses Bird, each clutching a glass of sherry and looking a trifle uncomfortable in large, western-style hats.

'Good evening, Father,' they said as one.

'Good evening, ladies.'

'I hope the entertainment isn't too rowdy for you,' continued Mavis, the slightly taller of the two and my ally at the ecumenical discussion group. 'We don't really like the music, but we feel we want to support the parish.'

'Yes,' said the other, 'even though the money *is* going towards the reordering. We think you were absolutely right about that, Father.'

'Yes, we do,' said her sister.

It was a bit like watching a game of tennis, and I felt my neck straining with the effort to keep up.

'Well, we're stuck with it now,' I said. 'I only hope the builders do a good job.'

'Are you really going to throw babies into that awful pool.'

'I don't see I have any choice.'

'How horrible. Perhaps they'll learn to swim.'

The thought that some use might come of the pool after all seemed to cheer them a bit and they accepted my offer of another sherry.

'We do like the Latin Masses,' said the smaller Bird.

'Oh, yes,' said the other. 'I never really liked it when they brought the English in. In, fact I still prefer the old Mass.'

'You don't belong to WAR!, then, ladies?'

They looked horror-struck at the very suggestion and began to criticise Lavender Buller and all her works in very round terms. It seemed that they had only joined the Liturgy Planning Group because they wanted to 'help the parish out' and in the early stages had been rather browbeaten by Buller, Phillips and my modernist predecessor, an absolutely killer combination. Now that I was here they were much happier and hoped that I would continue with my plans of going 'forward to the past.'

'I'll do my best,' I said, 'but you have to realise what I'm up against.'

'Oh, we do,' they said, as one. 'We've had to put up with it ourselves for years. Perhaps you can force the WAR! ladies to go off and bother another parish.'

They tottered off and I looked around to see if Julia had come. I spotted her near the front of the hall talking to some of her colleagues from the school, her figure very well set off by the country and western costume and making her look, as usual, like a model who had strayed into everyday life. Of Spooner there was no sign. Before long, the evening developed into a karaoke session, the Nurdles providing the music while parishioners got up and sang the words of songs displayed on a screen by the far wall. O'Grady didn't waste much time before availing himself of this opportunity, ignoring the songs available and launching into some Irish ballad that sent everyone off to the bar. I ordered another pint before the mob hit me, and was disturbed to find Tonks at my elbow urging me to participate.

'Come on, Jim,' he said. 'It's just a bit of fun. Here, have a look at this list. You must know some of them.'

149

I did indeed, but was disinclined to join in, feeling a little shy of performing in front of the parishioners. I was therefore relieved when Tonks went back to the band, but horrified when seconds later he announced my name.

'Come on, Jim,' he boomed through the microphone, slurring the words slightly and obviously a little drunk. 'You know you want to.'

I shook my head, but there was a huge round of applause from the mob and they all seemed to expect me to get up. At this point Dermot Byrne came from nowhere and dragged me from my stool.

'Come on, laddie,' he said. 'You've no choice – it's traditional.'

Realising I was beaten, I moved towards the stage to another huge round of applause and quickly consulted the songbook again. After a brief perusal, I told Tonks I would sing *My Way*.

'Good choice,' he said. 'Oddly enough, Father Hicks always used to go for that one.'

In the end, I enjoyed my five minutes of fame and returned to the bar to yet more applause and a good deal of back-slapping. Afterwards, everyone wanted to buy me a drink and I was surrounded by a knot of parishioners whom I barely knew, congratulating me on my singing and asking me if I had any more surprises in store for the parish after Christmas. I wasn't quite sure whether they were referring to my liturgical changes or my singing, but told them that they shouldn't think I was finished yet. A few of them urged me not to give up and, like the Misses Bird, said how sorry they were at the way I had been treated over the reordering. I saw the Bullers eyeing me during these conversations and wondered whether they were anxious I might return after the Christmas break with further challenges to their borrowed authority. In this was so, I reflected, they were right.

SEVENTEEN

I flew to Montpellier on Boxing Day, delighted to be able to get away from the wretched Christmas Masses that had blighted the preceding days. Tonks, despite his increased friendliness towards me, had gone into overdrive and the music was as inappropriate as ever. To his credit, O'Grady had finally got around to producing a workable servers' rota, but I did not enjoy the Midnight Mass at all and was glad when it was over. The only good thing to come out of it was the reappearance of Spooner with the girl from the website, a slim, quiet-looking person with glasses who seemed much more the type that he should be looking for. He appeared content and I hoped that they would still be seeing each other when I got back. The fact that they were holding hands after the Mass and able to share a joke or two with me about the music boded well and I wished them a happy Christmas with some optimism. I'd been planning to ask whether Spooner wanted to have Christmas Day lunch with me and Terry Molloy, but formed the impression that this would be unnecessary. In the end, Terry and I were joined by Canon Taylor, with the latter's sister doing the cooking, an excellent arrangement.

The monastery turned out to be all I had expected, though the cold of the place was a little disconcerting. I slept a good deal, said my Mass in the old rite every day and attended the offices of the monks in the abbey church. My French is limited, but I can hold a conversation and was able to explain to the guest-master the troubles I was having in my parish. He assured me that things in France were much worse and that traditionalists like themselves were not at all popular with the rest of the clergy. Vocations in the dioceses were at an all time low, the modernist rot was everywhere and only places like Notre Dame-de-Monts were flourishing. I could see why, for the spirit among the young monks was impressive and the prayerfulness and calm of the place highly edifying. I had plenty of time for reading and continued thinking about what I would do when I got back to the parish.

With Christmas over, I was now freed from the promise I had made to Sloane not to change things until after the new year. However, did I really want to upset the status quo again? As the parish social had shown, I was now reasonably popular among the people and they seemed to like the settlement that had been reached. Why should I risk everything by making any further changes? If I did so, I knew it wouldn't be long before the Buller/Phillips axis got busy again and this time, without a shadow of a doubt, the bishop would lose patience and pack me off to whatever Siberia he had lined up for recalcitrant clergy. Since I was still only in my thirties, I didn't want to turn into another Terry Molloy and spend the rest of my years festering in a backwater, knowing that I had failed to achieve any of the aims I now had. Perhaps it would be better to lie low and wait for another bishop to come along who might do things differently. I remained convinced that the modernist experiment had failed and that sooner or later the Church would have to return to more traditional practices. Why force the issue now when perhaps people weren't ready for it?

On the other hand, could I live with myself if I took the option of meekly going along with the wishes of those more powerful than myself, wishes I was sure were contrary to the good of the Church? It was quite clear that there was a very real battle going on, a battle between the out and out progressives like Sloane and the Bullers and traditionalists like myself. People such as Canon Taylor and Terry Molloy who had tried to take a middle path had simply been frozen out, and I was convinced that in the end I would be too. After all, despite all my efforts we still had the ecumenical discussion groups and the reordering, not to mention the 'folk' music, the Liturgy Planning Group and other vehicles of dissent. Some of these things, of course, if properly led, could have been quite valuable, but unless power were wrested from the WAR!

152

faction, I knew I had no chance. I had been allowed to get away with the odd Latin Mass during the week, but where it really counted the enemy were still in charge. As far as status quos went, this was not an especially favourable one and once the reordering was complete things would only get worse. No, I had to fight, and to fight meant bringing the battle to the opposition. Refreshed and invigorated by my time in the monastery, I would be able to begin in earnest the second phase on my attack on the forces of liberalism.

On returning to Cheeseminster, I found that the builders were hard at work again after their new year break and were busily smashing up the part of the church where the baptismal pool would eventually be inserted. Trying to put this vandalism out of my mind, I decided that the first thing to do was to prepare the parishioners for my next traditionalist *putsch* and announce in the weekly newsletter certain changes for the following week. These would comprise all Masses on weekdays being in Latin and the introduction of a regular Benediction of the Blessed Sacrament on Sunday afternoons. This ceremony, common in most parishes up until the Council, had been almost completely abandoned, but I was determined to persuade O'Grady to lend me a handful of servers to make it work. It involved the adoration of the Blessed Sacrament as well as certain hymns and prayers, the kind of thing that the Sloanes of this world would not have touched with a bargepole. Furthermore, the ceremony was largely in Latin.

Trouble was not long in coming. When the newsletter went out the following Sunday, it created a major stir and I was informed by Buller that the WAR! Council would be meeting to consider what action to take.

'I knew no good would come of your going to that French abbey,' she said, in her haughtiest manner. 'Try to remember what happened the last time you pulled a stunt like this. The *Cheeseminster Echo* is only a phone-call away and we have many ladies in the group who are prepared to come large distances to demonstrate. Furthermore, you must know the considerable influence I have with the bishop. In short, I would advise you to think again.'

The aftermath was as predictable as it was tedious, a re-run of what had happened when I first introduced the Latin Masses. The demonstrators duly arrived, about twenty of them, and a report appeared in the paper. I decided to strike back by asking the *Echo* if I could write an article for the *Fromage Faith* column explaining my position, and was rewarded with the promise of a full page interview in which I could outline my views on Latin Masses and more besides. As soon as this appeared I received a call from Sloane.

'The bishop and I need to see you again,' he said, dryly.

I could tell he was far from pleased. This time the meeting was a good deal less cordial than before.

'Now listen, James,' said Sloane, after ushering me into the bishop's presence. 'This can't go on. We want you to reintroduce the English Masses.'

'Yes,' said the bishop, looking rather worn out, as if my actions were the last straw. I knew he had been under a lot of pressure in the local press recently over a priest who had been convicted of a child abuse offence and probably thought that the waves I was causing were in very bad taste. 'I felt that the compromise introduced when Monsignor Sloane was in residence was working well. Why spoil things with this extremism?'

'I do not consider it extremism, bishop,' I replied, already a little hot under the collar. 'What I consider extreme are unnecessary reorderings and dissenting groups such as We Are Right! This time, I propose to do what *I* feel is right. I would like to know whether you intend to tell Lavender Buller that she is the cause of the problems in the parish, not me?'

The bishop was so astonished at my forthrightness that he seemed incapable of speech. Sloane was not so easily ruffled.

'You really believe in turning the clock back like this?' he said.

'I wouldn't put it like that, but I do believe that what I'm doing is right.'

'And do you intend to make any further changes?'

'Yes.'

'Such as?'

'Latin Masses on Sundays.'

'I see.'

There was one further thing I didn't mention, but it was something I knew he would hate almost as much. This was to deliver a series of talks on the sexual teachings of the Church, emphasising such things as the need for married couples to follow Church teaching on the inadmissibility of artificial contraception. This would probably create a furore at least as great as the storm over the Masses, but I felt moved to do it to counter the almost universal silence on this issue that reigned in the diocese. For reasons that I cannot quite fathom even now, I had become increasingly concerned during my time in the seminary that what was in fact a coherent and logical body of teaching had been swept under the carpet or vilified by those opposed to it. Since I felt capable of giving a well-informed series of talks on the subject, it seemed my duty to do so and one that I could not put off just because of the reaction I might get from Buller and Sloane, not to mention Tonks and numerous others. However, I decided not to tell Sloane about this now as it seemed we had enough on our plate that afternoon with purely liturgical questions. At this point, Sloane appeared to change tack.

'Would you like a cup of tea, James?' he asked.

'Why not?'

'And a biscuit?'

'Thank you.'

He disappeared and the bishop began to make small talk about the fortunes of Gorgehampton Wanderers. I wondered what on earth was going to happen next, perhaps a James Bond-style poisoning by means of the tea or a summary dismissal from my duties in the parish. Eventually, all became clear.

'I believe you had old Canon Taylor over for lunch at Christmas,' said the bishop, on Sloane's return.

'Yes,' I replied, still somewhat surprised by the turn the conversation had taken.

'Did the Canon mention his imminent departure from the Muckford nursing home?'

'He did. He said his health was still bad and that his sister was now going to look after him.'

'Did he tell you when this was happening?'

'The middle of next month.'

At this point Sloane took up the baton.

'As you can imagine,' he said, stirring his tea and switching on one of his most self-satisfied smiles, 'it's been rather hard finding a replacement. You know the shortage of priests we have in this diocese and it's not a post everyone would want. When the bishop and I discussed this, the only person we could think of to fill the post was you.'

It was obvious now where this was leading.

'Yes,' continued the bishop. 'Your name came up quite early in the discussion. Monsignor Sloane's view was that, after all the stress and strain you've been under at Cheeseminster, you would probably welcome a quiet appointment like that, a good place to say your Latin Masses and a chance to get ahead with all the reading you seem to like doing. The monsignor thought you'd jump at it.'

Sloane continued to smile, though far from benevolently.

'Those were my thoughts exactly,' he said. 'Of course, if things were to settle down in Cheeseminster one doubts whether such an upheaval would be worth it, but the bishop and I are now wondering quite seriously whether they ever will.'

So, that was it. I would be sent to Muckford in the middle of February unless I restored the status quo. At least, I reflected, they had made the situation clear and I knew now what my fate would be if I carried on upsetting them. There only remained to decide what to do and as I drove back to

Cheeseminster I pondered whether I was prepared to betray my principles a second time and become the time-serving cleric they wanted.

Without too much hesitation, I decided I could not.

EIGHTEEN

For a while, the demonstrations continued. I admired the old ladies who were prepared to turn up quite early in the morning to wave their fists at me as I unlocked the hall and unfurl a banner reading 'WE ARE RIGHT AND WE WILL FIGHT!' They tended to hang around until the Mass was over and then take the number nine bus back to Gorgehampton. One morning, I invited them in to attend the Mass they so vehemently despised, suggesting that they might get to like it if they gave it a chance, but they seemed disinclined to take up the offer. In fact, they burst into a chorus of *We Shall Not be Moved*, so I decided to leave them to it. Later on, I issued an invitation for coffee at the presbytery, but I could see they were anxious not to miss the bus. What was particularly gratifying to note was that apart from Phillips and the Bullers, the only person from the parish who ever appeared was Tonks, who turned up one morning looking very uncomfortable and disappeared before the end of Mass. This was the same morning that Drone arrived with a counter-demonstration by members of the Campaign for Real Catholicism, consisting of three old men and a dog. It was all most bizarre.

I now noticed a split developing in my enemies' ranks. Tonks rang me to say that Buller had ordered a renewed policy of non-cooperation and that therefore he was pulling out his choir from next Sunday's Mass. Since I was about to sack him anyway and replace him with Mrs. Moss, this was, almost literally, music to my ears, and I heard him out with some glee. Mrs. Moss agreed to bring her Gregorian choir to the eleven o'clock, which was henceforth going to contain a great deal more Latin than English. I asked her why she wasn't demonstrating with the other WAR! members, but she said she had resigned after a row with Lavender Buller about the music.

O'Grady, meanwhile, seemed wholly to have come over to my side. He had increasingly resented the encroachment of Tonks' choir members into the makeshift sanctuary at the hall and the two of them had apparently almost come to blows on the Sunday when I was in France. When I told him that Tonks was no longer co-operating with me, he informed me that, despite Buller's firm injunction, he would not pull his lads out, merely his girls. The girls, he said, had reacted badly to the rota he had drawn up and he had been forced to discipline them for dissent. At this point their parents had rung him and told him where he could stick his altar-serving, a move that had solved the overcrowding problems at a stroke. I now hastily arranged a meeting with O'Grady and the boys, who seemed delighted by the absence of their female counterparts, and schooled them in the requirements for serving a sung Latin Mass. I was gratified to see that this went down well. The fact that I would now be saying the eleven o'clock facing east meant that I could move the portable altar back a long way, thus providing much more space for the kind of intricate choreography that would be required. I also introduced the thurible, previously banned by O'Grady, and explained that one boy would be responsible for lighting charcoal and swinging the thing backwards and forwards to keep it alight. This went down very well indeed, so I moved rapidly on to a rehearsal for Benediction of the Blessed Sacrament, also involving lots of smoke and movement. By the time I had finished, the boys were fighting for who would do the most important jobs, a headache that I left O'Grady to sort out while writing my next newsletter, explaining the latest changes.

The Sunday I had chosen for the full programme of Latin Masses also turned out to be the Sunday of the monthly CRC Mass. I was therefore left with a very busy schedule, but since, if Sloane were true to his word, I would soon be in retirement over at Muckford, notions of tiredness hardly seemed relevant. I awoke early, but not early enough to avoid Miranda Phillips, who had just driven into the car-park with three WAR! members. I greeted them heartily, trying to show that I bore them no ill will, but Phillips merely glared at me and directed her fellow warriors to their positions in front of the hall. A little later I looked out and saw that the Bullers and Tonks had arrived with more demonstrators, who promptly unfurled their 'WE ARE RIGHT AND WE WILL FIGHT!' banner and fixed it above the main entrance to the hall. I felt this could only backfire on them. It was clear, judging by the comments I had received over the last week, that most of the parishioners viewed them as a lunatic fringe and that the level of support I enjoyed was much greater than I had suspected. A few people had come up to me and told me quite politely that they would never set foot in the church again until the English Masses were restored, but by and large the majority had taken it all in their stride. I had explained carefully in the newsletter that booklets with English translations would be provided and most had seemed satisfied with that. Many had enjoyed my interview in the *Echo* and it was clear that the various demonstrations were seen as an embarrassment, largely perpetrated by outsiders.

Fortunately, the demonstrators decided not to sing during the eight o'clock, a simple, low Mass with no music or frills. However, as the congregation emerged afterwards they pressed leaflets on them explaining the dangers of neo-traditionalism and how I was an agent of fear and obscurantism who wished to see the laity silent and in chains. It was heady stuff and I was pleased later on to see most of the leaflets stuffed in the bin in the car-park. I went into breakfast, but at this point the chanting began and I was obliged to turn on the radio to drown it out. Occasionally I heard snatches of various Tonks-like hymns and the twang of the man himself accompanying them on the guitar. When I re-emerged I was greeted by the reporter who had interviewed me for the *Echo*, accompanied by a broadcasting team from Gorge TV, who asked me if I would answer a few questions. Reflecting how much this would annoy a media creature like Sloane, I agreed and looked forward to seeing the interview on the local news that evening. I then entered the hall to prepare for the big event.

The television crew were not disappointed by what happened. O'Grady and I carefully prepared the procession in the hall kitchen and then emerged in stately fashion as Mrs. Moss struck up the Gregorian choir. It was my plan, as usual, to take the servers round the side of the building and in through the front door, entering as the choir reached its climax. I had got rid of the Moroccan outfits and replaced them with traditional cassocks and cottas that had been stowed away by my predecessor in a strongbox. As we reached the demonstrators they started chanting 'We are right and we will fight!' and I thought for a minute that they were going to try and bar the entry of the procession into the hall. What actually happened was even more dramatic, for I was just in time to spot a flying egg, hurled by one of the more militant members, sailing towards my head. I ducked and it hit the reporter from the *Echo* full in the face. This was terrific. Then we pushed through the mob and passed peacefully into the hall, though not before one of the servers had been jostled by a couple of burly women, an action that was caught by the television camera.

Once inside, all proceeded smoothly. The servers had been well drilled by O'Grady and few mistakes were made. The choir was in good voice and some of the older members of the congregation joined lustily in the singing. At the end of the Mass, I announced the beginning of a series of talks on 'Catholicism and Sex', before forming up the servers and processing out again into the sunlight of a crisp winter's day. I hung around as usual to greet the congregation as they came out and was gratified by a succession of supportive remarks from parishioners, some of whom turned to the demonstrators and muttered things like 'shame on you' and 'you're a disgrace.' Not many leaflets were handed out after that and I soon saw Buller and company packing up their banner in subdued mood.

If this was a war, then the first victory was mine. The television report later that day was the icing on the cake. There were excellent shots, both of the egg exploding on the reporter's face and the jostling of the altar boys, and Buller came across as suitably fanatical in her interview. That evening I received quite a few supportive phone calls, though my usual critics among the diocesan clergy also wanted to have their say. Pleasingly, the Beast rang up to support me, declaring that he had never seen anything quite so amusing on television for years, while Canon Taylor and Terry Molloy also voiced encouragement for the stand I was taking. Sloane, I knew, was in London, so was unlikely to have heard about these events yet. He had been rushed up by the BBC to deliver his initial *Thought for the Day* and was due to be in London for some time, making an episode for a television programme entitled *Priests Who Stray*, about the current paedophilia crisis. Before going to bed, I reflected on the afternoon's activities, which had been a lot more peaceful. Many of those who had attended the eleven o'clock made a day of it and also attended the CRC Mass and Benediction. Several came up to me at the end of it all and shook me warmly by the hand, practically in tears. They said that they had never thought to see tradition restored in the Catholic Church and encouraged me to fight with all the energy at my disposal to continue what I was doing.

There was no let-up the following day and the phone rang constantly with people from all over the region reacting to what they had seen on their televisions the night before. I could see that there was already a danger that I would become a cult figure and was worried now that it might all get hopelessly out of hand. The bishop, however, remained silent, seemingly helpless without Sloane to tell him what to do. If he telephoned, I knew what my reply would be, but the call did not come. I therefore proceeded with my usual routine and was gratified to see that no demonstrators appeared to disrupt the Monday morning Mass. Furthermore, attendance was up and I was pleased to see Spooner turn up once again with the girl, whom this time he introduced as Isobel Quigley. She came out of her shell to the extent of expressing her gushing support for what I was doing and saying that she and Spooner had just taken out joint membership of the CRC. Now that he was in a 'steady' relationship, Spooner had practically stopped ringing me, for which I was most grateful, and the name of Julia never passed his lips. This was all very much to the good and I hoped his lunatic days with women were over.

Monday was supposed to be my day off, but I wanted to have a word with Julia about making the school Mass more traditional and therefore went over to the staff-room for morning break. She was gushing in her support for my actions and the cupboard became our home again as she asked me what was going to happen about the *Dogma and Doctrine* question. This was the one area where I felt powerless. Sloane had warned me not to interfere and I knew that I would never be able to persuade the powers that be in the school to defy the diocesan bureaucracy. This was how Julia read the question as well, but she had an answer to it.

'Do you have, say, thirty copies of *Dogma and Doctrine* at the presbytery?' she asked.

'Yes,' I said, somewhat perplexed as to where this was leading. 'I ordered them when I thought we had a chance of doing something.'

'Good, because I intend to use them with my class.'

'But that will get you into a lot of trouble.'

'I don't care about that. You're sticking your neck out to get things changed at the church, so I want to do my bit here. I'll start using the book and see what happens.'

I told her I admired her courage, but suggested that she had her career to consider.

'That's true,' she said, 'but what's the point of having a career like that, where you're forced to water down the truth until it's insipid. I learned nothing about the Catholic faith at school and I don't want these children to go through the same, pointless process. I'll come and get the books at lunchtime.'

163

I was encouraged by all this but very anxious for her. It was all very well for me to be reckless, but she was a young teacher with a long future ahead of her. However, when I argued with her again later she was adamant and insisted on taking the books.

Wednesday night was to be the occasion of my first 'Catholics and Sex' talk. Anticipating a large audience, I got O'Grady and Spooner to help me re-arrange the hall and moved the Blessed Sacrament into the presbytery. Everything went according to plan. A reporter came from the *Echo*, Buller, Phillips and Tonks turned up to ask awkward questions, and Julia, Drone and others to ask helpful ones. I felt sure of my ground in this area because of all the reading I had done over the years and hoped to show that the Church, in advocating sexual abstinence at times when the secular world was pushing its opposite, was not simply issuing a set of prohibitive commands but proposing a coherent theology of married love. Intending to give four talks in all, I was anxious to stick to the limited remit I had given myself that evening, but inevitably the discussion turned to wider issues and Buller and co. wanted to know what I felt about all the usual hot topics. We therefore discussed birth control, premarital sex, homosexuality and other favourites and I was able to show why the Church had adopted the positions it had on these issues. Needless to say, my opponents affected to be shocked that I could possibly be supportive of such 'repressive' attitudes and declared that sooner or later all this would change and the Church would fall into line with secular opinion. This gave me a chance to quote the dictum that 'he who marries the spirit of the age is likely to end a widower' and the evening ended with tea and biscuits. All in all, then, I felt it an excellent start to what I hoped would be an eye-opener for quite a few people in the parish, though I was disappointed by how few young people were present. Since most of the children who passed through the school lapsed from the faith as soon as they entered their teens, if not sooner, this was, however, not really surprising.

A few days later Julia reported that there had indeed been a stink about the use of the new textbooks. Her frightened boss had ordered her to go back to *Look at Me, Lord* and Julia had refused. As yet, the issue had not become a disciplinary matter, but I wondered how long things could remain like that. As chairman of the school governors I did, of course, have some clout and wondered how I could use it to support what Julia was doing. It seemed clear that a meeting would have to be called and I arranged one for the following week, the object being to discuss the two textbooks and decide which one the majority of the governors preferred. This might not solve anything, but at least it would buy Julia some time and I managed to persuade her to drop *Dogma and Doctrine* at least until we had had the meeting.

Things were hotting up.

(NINETEEN)

The following Sunday, the WAR! demonstrators changed tack. This time they held banners saying 'THE DEATH OF FREEDOM' and 'WE ACCUSE JAMES PAGE' and had all dressed in black. As the procession entered the church at eleven o'clock they began to hum mournfully, swaying from side to side and waving candles. It was all most disturbing and they had come in numbers, We Are Right! supporters having been bussed in from all the surrounding areas. Once again the majority of parishioners ignored them, but the television cameras were there and a brief report appeared on that evening's news. This time I did hear from the bishop, but before he had a chance to speak I said my piece.

'Bishop, I demand that you speak to Lavender Buller and get her to remove her demonstrators.'

'That is not the issue,' he replied, clearly flustered.

'I think it is. Without the demonstrators the television would have nothing to film. Buller is making a spectacle of the parish and the Church in your diocese.'

There was a pause at the other end of the line and I wondered how he would respond.

'She has a right to protest if she feels strongly enough,' he said, finally.

'Why not condemn WAR! and all their works?' I replied. 'You must know that they dissent from a lot of Church teaching.'

'I would not put it like that.'

'I don't know how else you could put it.'

There was another pause. The conversation was clearly not going as he had expected.

'Look, James,' he said, evidently making a last ditch attempt to win me round. 'You must know that you only have a month to go in your parish now. Why not go quietly?'

166

'I cannot do other than what I believe to be right.'

'This is all most regrettable,' he sighed.

He sounded in the pit of despair and I almost began to feel sorry for him. Without Sloane he really was just the victim of events. He rang off and I knew that there was no question now that Muckford would be my next port of call as a priest. For the moment, however, I had other things to think about.

The parish as a whole was continuing to react well to the various changes and the early evening Benediction had once again attracted quite a crowd. Most people seemed happy to kneel at the altar rails at Mass and receive communion on the tongue, a practice that was aided by my training an altar boy to go along the rails with me holding a communion plate. When they saw the plate, even the waverers tended to lower their hands and since the WAR! group were now attending Mass elsewhere I did not have any trouble from them.

My second sexuality talk was as well attended as the first, and since my main topic this time was the joys of natural methods of birth control, I made sure that plenty of leaflets were available promoting the practice. I had just read about a very reliable natural method that had recently been developed and had ordered a gross of booklets on the subject, as well as listing places where the method could be learnt and the name of the organisation that had developed it. This speech went down a storm, despite relentless barracking from the usual suspects, and many expressed their amazement that reliable natural methods existed at all. So many people had been brought up on notions of 'Vatican roulette' that they were unaware that things had moved on since the sixties, and I received a lot of comments along the lines of 'Why has nobody told us about this before?' This was all most gratifying, as was a telephone call later in the week from the organisation I had promoted, telling me they had been inundated with calls.

The school governors' meeting was another matter. I had circulated copies of both *Dogma and Doctrine* and *Look*

167

At Me, Lord to the governing body beforehand and had invited them to comment on which they thought was more suitable for use in a Catholic school. I said nothing myself as to which I preferred, but found that the opinion was overwhelmingly in favour of the former. I don't think that many of the governors had ever looked closely at *Look At Me, Lord* before and had no idea how useless it really was. However, unluckily for me word had got out that the diocesan bureaucracy was in love with it and such was the fear of crossing that august body that, when a vote was taken, they decided that it might be more prudent to carry on with what we had already. This led naturally to the question of what we were going to do about Julia and, in a move that was at least logical given what they had already decided, it was overwhelmingly felt that she should be asked to toe the line. When I informed Julia of this that evening she exploded.

'What pathetic cowards they are,' she said, barely able to control herself.

'I think you'd better go along with it,' I said. 'We've made our point.'

'You might have, Father. I haven't even started yet.'

'But you might get suspended.'

'Stuff their suspension.'

I had never expected Julia to get so worked up about the issue and now regretted ever showing her the books. If anybody around the parish was going to be a martyr, it was going to be me and I had no real wish to take others down with me. I hoped she would be in a calmer frame of mind in the morning, but when I went over to the school the next day found that she was busily teaching from *Dogma and Doctrine* again. I knew now that her doom could not be far off.

The following Sunday may well rank as one of the most bizarre in my life and proved to be the day when matters finally came to a head. I was surprised, on going over to the hall, that the demonstrators appeared not to have turned up, but as the procession entered the building at the beginning of Mass I found that the place was fuller than it had ever been.

To say that it was standing room only would be an understatement and as I plodded down the aisle I recognised most of my old foes. Everyone was dressed normally this time, but my feeling that the calm could not last proved correct. At the very moment the procession arrived at the altar rails a cry of 'Down with the oppressors!' went up and several pink balloons were released into the congregation. I was told later that they were not balloons at all, but balloons were what they looked like to me at the time. Then the habitual demonstrators began to chant 'We are one, we are one, we are right and you are wrong!' before regrouping in the aisle and processing out in a gaggle. Fortunately, the old codger who plays the organ turned up the volume at this point and I could not hear the rest of their song. Trying to appear unruffled, though ruffled I was, I carried on the Mass as if nothing had happened while O'Grady went round the hall retrieving the 'balloons'. As we processed out at the end of Mass I noticed my friends, the television crew, in action once again and Lavender Buller giving her customary interview. I then had a chance to make my own comments before retiring, shattered and bemused, to the presbytery.

At three o'clock that afternoon, Sloane arrived.

'See what you've done?' he said, his cool evidently having been misplaced somewhere between Gorgehampton and Cheeseminster.

'What *I've* done,' I replied, unable to believe what I was hearing.

'You can't deny responsibility. You were warned off and you continued your ridiculous experiments.'

I wasn't going to take this.

'If you'd told Buller to get a grip on herself,' I said, 'none of this would have happened.'

For a second he actually looked a trifle sheepish, not an emotion I had ever seen in him before.

'I did speak to Lavender,' he said, 'but she wouldn't listen. She said she had been provoked beyond endurance and I could see her point.'

'That's absurd.'

We argued this for some time before I asked him what he intended to do. He was evidently very annoyed, having had to cut short his filming in London after an anxious call from the bishop had summoned him back to the diocese. I now learned that I would once again have him as my guest.

'In a few weeks' time,' he said, 'you will be off to Muckford and your successor, whoever he may be, will take over. In the meantime I intend to remain here and restore order. The bishop has had more than he can take from you and if he has a nervous breakdown it will be your fault.'

At this point I left him, unable to stand such nonsense any longer. I decided to go straight out to the suburbs and consult Terry Molloy and together we watched a Gorge TV bulletin about inflated condoms being let off during Mass at the Cheeseminster Catholic church. Terry thought this was hugely funny, but became more serious when I explained that Sloane had arrived to put an end to my traditionalist revolution.

'Are you going to put up with him this time?' he asked.

'I don't see I have any choice. I can't kick him out.'

'No. But there's a way forward you might not have considered.'

Terry now outlined to me a plan that was so brilliant yet so obvious I wondered why I hadn't thought of it before.

'Mind you,' he said, 'if you do this, you can kiss good-bye to Muckford. Would that bother you?'

'Not really. I never wanted to go there at all.'

'Right. Well, I think you should go ahead. Don't worry, I'll help you out. I also know that, if it comes to the crunch, the Beast will give you his support, as will Canon Taylor. You aren't completely alone, you know.'

I thanked him for these words of comfort and told him I would put the plan into effect that very evening.

After a dreary supper back at the presbytery, during which we hardly spoke, Sloane and I went our separate ways.

He had already outlined what he wanted from me, this being a return to the pre-Christmas status quo, to last until I had left for Muckford. He would remain until then to 'help me out'. I told him that the parishioners had moved on liturgically since Christmas and had largely accepted my changes, but he wouldn't listen and merely commented that he would be saying Mass, in English, the following morning in the hall.

Having retired to my room I began preparations for putting Terry's plan into action, packing a suitcase, a camp bed, some cooking equipment and various other items vital to my personal well-being. I then walked over to the church and unlocked the sacristy, having ensured that I had taken both sets of keys. Depositing what I had brought, I used a torch to have a look around the interior, not wishing to alert Sloane to my presence there as yet. I wanted the events of the following day to come as a surprise. The builders, as I had suspected, had not yet done a great deal of work, the main focus of interest so far being the rear of the nave where the baptismal pool was going to be placed. The sanctuary was as yet untouched. As for chairs, there were still quite a few around as the hall had largely been filled with ones from the school. In short, Mass with a congregation could be celebrated with ease, so long as the builders weren't there.

I now returned to the sacristy and telephoned all the regular members of the morning Mass congregation. I informed them that the next day's Mass would be half an hour earlier than normal and would, unusually, take place in the church. I then made up my bed and prepared for a good night's sleep. The real revolution had begun.

TWENTY

Everything went according to plan and Sloane was greeted with the sight of the congregation leaving my Mass just as he was preparing to start his. I had explained to them that each morning I would be saying an old rite Mass in Latin in the church, not the new rite one I had used before. If they didn't like the sound of this they could always go to Sloane's Mass in the hall half an hour later. Margaret Bird had asked me if I had the bishop's approval for this and I had to confess that I did not. I argued, however, that the old Mass had never been abrogated by the Church and that it was up to them whether it mattered that I didn't have episcopal approval. One person left at this stage, but all the others stayed on. I had debated long and hard whether to take this extra step, but in the end had decided that my revolution, if it was going to be worthwhile, had better be as thoroughgoing as possible. I had already broken my bridges with the bishop, so in the end there was little left to lose. Drone, as the representative of the CRC, was the key figure here. I knew that it was the CRC's policy only to hold Masses approved by the bishops, so for him to support what I was doing would probably mean resigning from his post. He had assured me on the phone the night before, however, that he was right behind me and, so as not to compromise the CRC, he said he would resign that very evening. He even agreed to serve the Mass, a gesture I greatly appreciated.

When Sloane saw his congregation disappearing down the drive, he came across and asked what the hell was going on. I explained that I had rung up the builders and told them that work on the church was suspended, my aim being to use the building to say a daily and Sunday old rite Mass. At this point Sloane made various insulting remarks about my sanity and asked me to give him the keys to the church. I refused. He then gave me an ultimatum. Either I stopped what I was doing and moved out of the church or he would call the police. Now, I am not very well up on the laws about squatting and such like, but I somehow felt that in the cold light of day Sloane would realise that he would be wasting his time if he tried to do this. Furthermore, I told him now that if he did do so I would ensure that the press were there to report it. His desire to avoid scandal was usually the uppermost thought in his mind, and if he could keep my rebellion in-house he would undoubtedly do so. The whole point of his coming to Cheeseminster a second time had been to put an end to the seemingly endless newspaper and television reports about the parish, so it seemed unlikely that he would risk further coverage. In the end he stormed off, muttering to himself, and I wondered what would happen next.

Having prepared breakfast in the sacristy on the camp-stove I had brought with me, I settled down to read a book and awaited developments. Before long there was a bang on the door and I was greeted by the sight of the Beast of Chedderford pushing Canon Taylor in a wheelchair, with Terry Molloy not far behind. I invited them in. The Beast practically punched me to the floor, evidently his idea of an affectionate greeting.

'Don't worry,' he said. 'We've seen Sloane. You won't get any more trouble from him.'

'Why not?'

'Because Terry and I have said that we'll say Latin Masses in our parishes and go the press about it if he starts anything.'

'Thanks a lot,' I said, immensely grateful for this.

'Yes,' said Terry. 'I might say a Latin Mass or two anyway, just to annoy him.'

They asked me if I was enjoying my new living accommodation and handed me a Sainsbury's bag full of provisions. I told them that the church was rather cold and asked if they could bring me a heater of some kind. Terry had already thought of that and now brought one from his car, saying that if I felt like going out once in a while he would be happy to occupy the church for me. Not long after their departure I received a visit from the Misses Bird.

'Are you sure you'll be all right, Father?' said Mavis.

I assured her that I would be fine and that the best thing they could do would be to turn up for Mass the next day at the same time. I could see, however, that they were keen to do something further, so I suggested that a hot meal every now and again would not go amiss. This request cheered them enormously and they hurried off to produce something for lunch. Next in was Julia, who came across from the school during morning break. She seemed rather agitated.

'Anything wrong?' I asked.

'Yes. It looks as if the suspension will go through. I had a major row with the head this morning.'

'I'm sorry.'

'Don't be. They can stick their silly job. I'm only upset for the children, who'll never understand what's going on.'

She looked round the sacristy, evidently not greatly impressed by my new home.

'How long do you think you'll be staying here?' she asked.

I pondered this, not having looked that far ahead.

'No idea, really. My long term aims are rather fuzzy. I'll tell you when I've worked them out.'

'Well, good luck anyway, Father. I must get back to the school.'

She left in a hurry and by the end of the day, despite an excellent lunch provided by the Birds, I was beginning to feel rather fed up. Fortunately, however, that evening Drone arrived with some good news from his members.

'They're all behind you,' he said. 'We're actually forming a breakaway group called the Gorgehampton Traditionalists. Not very snappy, I know, but the best we could do off the top of our heads. I've issued a three-line whip for Sunday. Everybody should be here. As I see it, what we ought

174

to aim for is getting more people to your Mass than to Monsignor Sloane's.'

I asked him if he thought the press had got wind of what was happening. I didn't want to cause more trouble for the diocese than was necessary and hoped that if possible the whole thing could be kept relatively low-key. Drone thought this was rather a lot to hope for, but said he would try and find out through his contacts how widely news of my stand had spread.

My last visitor of the day was Sloane. He came in looking thoroughly fed up and I asked whether he had decided to give up and go back to Gorgehampton.

'Not at all,' he said, 'but I do have a message from the bishop. He would like to see you.'

My answer to that was clear.

'I have nothing further to say to him. If he really wants to talk, he can ring me.'

Sloane gave me a pitying look.

'Don't be a fool, James. Have you considered the damage this row is doing to the diocese, not to mention your own career? It still isn't too late to draw back, you know.'

I told him that the idea of Muckford no longer appealed and he asked just how long I was intending to keep up what he called 'this charade'.

'You'll have to see.'

He stomped off and, after an unappetising meal of two pork pies and a scotch egg, I tried to get some sleep.

Mass the next morning was very well-attended, bringing with it much support from all present. Despite the fact that I had to get through it with a sore back, brought on by the decidedly sub-standard camp-bed, I returned to the sacristy in optimistic mood. The next thing that happened was much less welcome.

'Hello,' said a voice outside the window, just after I had finished breakfast.

'Who's there?'

'*Cheeseminster Echo*. We want to run another feature on you, Father Page.'

I groaned. How much had the *Echo* found out? I invited the fellow in and, to make sure that the record was straight about what I was doing, tried to explain why I had taken my stand. He seemed most interested in what I had to say and then disappeared off to the presbytery to get Sloane's angle on the story. The next thing that happened was a telephone call from the bishop. I knew it would come sooner or later, but it was no more agreeable for that. We now spent half an hour going round the houses, it being clear that he had no new offer to make and that I had not changed my position. The conversation ended with him muttering how sad he was that it had come to this, the first thing he had said that I could wholeheartedly agree with.

Terry now turned up to relieve me for half an hour and I went for a walk round the town. The first person I bumped into was Spencer White emerging from the Minster, who asked me what the hell was going on with the Catholics in Cheeseminster. I tried to explain.

'So you're in conflict with your bishop?' he said, when I had finished.

'Yes.'

'This is bad.'

'You don't have to tell me, Spencer.'

'Is there anything I can do for you?'

'Yes. Whatever you do, don't send Anthea Smith round for a chat.'

He found this terribly amusing and before moving off wished me well with the fight.

'I've no idea what you're trying to achieve,' he said, 'but good luck. Send me your address if you have to go away.'

As I headed back to the church, I fell into step with the slight figure of a woman I suddenly recognised as Spooner's girlfriend, Isobel. I asked if she had come to talk to me.

176

'Yes, that's just it,' she said, rather nervously. 'I need to ask you something about Mark.'

This sounded ominous. Spooner had been so quiet for so long I had almost forgotten about all his earlier problems, and the girl certainly looked anxious. I told her that if there was anybody who could help her with the Spooner question, it would be me. As soon as Terry had taken his leave, she burst into tears.

'I don't know what to do,' she said, after recovering her equilibrium a little. 'The thing is, Mark's asked me to marry him.'

This came as a considerable shock and I found it difficult to credit what I was hearing. Had he really decided to go down that road again? It was absurd. My next, rather unworthy reflection was that perhaps he was anxious to get some use out of the ring he had bought for Julia. I asked Isobel what she felt about this proposal.

'Well,' she said, rubbing her eyes, 'it's all so sudden. One minute we were just going out together, the next minute he was proposing. I mean, I've only known him just over a month.'

'I see the problem.'

This desperate desire of Spooner's to get married was incomprehensible to me. Was he worried that, when Isobel found out what he was really like, she might want to leave him? Was marriage a way of trapping her into a union from which she could not escape? I asked her what she had said when Spooner had proposed.

'I told him that I liked him, but that it was much too early to think about getting married.'

'How did he react?'

'He got drunk and asked me again.'

'And where did all this happen?'

'In a restaurant.'

I asked her whether Spooner was wearing a bow tie at the time of the proposal.

'Yes, how did you know?'

'Oh, just a guess.'

What was really troubling her, as it turned out, was that all this had happened on the Saturday night and she had not seen or heard from Spooner since. His phone was switched off and she was unable to visit him because she didn't know where he lived. My first reaction was to express surprise at this, but then I reflected that Spooner had probably been wise to keep her away from his flat. If anything was going to put the girl off him, it would be this. I asked her whether she was prepared to squat at the church while I went round to see if I could rouse her boyfriend.

'Would you really?' she said, evidently terribly relieved. 'I haven't been able to sleep for worrying.'

I reflected, as I walked round to Spooner's slum, that she was a much better person than he deserved and that he would be mad to do anything to put her off him. I was pretty certain I would find him in the flat and my instincts turned out to be correct.

'Mark,' I said, through the door, 'are you there? It's Father Page.'

I heard a shuffling sound within, accompanied by much fiddling with the lock, and eventually Spooner's head peered round the door. He looked appalling. His sparse, fair hair was greatly dishevelled and there were bags under his eyes. His skin was paler than ever and he gave off an odour of alcohol and sweat. He had not bothered to dress and was wearing faded pyjamas and a striped dressing-gown. I asked if I could come in and he nodded. The flat was, if anything, more untidy than at my last visit and empty beer cans were strewn everywhere. I noticed a whisky bottle lying on the floor, also empty, and scrunched-up crisp packets littered all over the chairs. I asked Spooner why he hadn't come to see me in his latest crisis and he explained that he had been too ashamed.

'I told you I loved Julia and now I've proposed to Isobel,' he moaned. 'You probably think I'm some kind of hypocrite.'

'Not at all.'

178

'I can't bear it. Why don't women like me?'

I thought he was going to burst into tears, but he contented himself with staring at the floor and rubbing his face with his hands. I tried to explain to him that Isobel liked him very much.

'She's very worried about you. Just because she doesn't want to marry you now doesn't mean to say she might not at some point in the future. You have to give these things time.'

After a while, he showed some signs of recovery and I told him to have a shave, get dressed and come round to the church. I didn't mention that Isobel was there, fearing he might not come if I did so, and in due course he appeared, still looking dreadful but better than before. When he saw his girlfriend he flinched a little and I thought he might run away, but fortunately he took his courage in his hands and the two of them had a long chat while I did a few jobs in the church. When I reappeared in the sacristy, all seemed to have been made up.

'We're going now, Father,' said Isobel, for whom I was beginning to have a high regard. 'Thank you very much for everything.'

'Yes, thanks,' said Spooner, looking rather embarrassed. 'Sorry for being so stupid.'

'Think nothing of it, Mark,' I said. 'It's made a welcome break to the routine.'

He began to look thoughtful.

'Do you want me to serve Mass tomorrow?' he asked.

'Why not? It'll do you good.'

What neither of us knew was that there would be no Mass.

•

179

I was awoken at seven by a terrible noise in the main body of the church and, after dressing hastily, entered to see several builders working away in the sanctuary. They were clearly trying to dismantle the old high altar and I blearily went over to remonstrate with them.

'Orders from Monsignor Sloane,' said the foreman. 'He wants us to start the work again.'

This was appalling.

'How did you get in?' I asked.

'A Mr. O'Grady gave us the key.'

So that was it. I had been betrayed by the snake in the grass O'Grady, whom I had come to see as an ally. No doubt Sloane had leaned heavily on him and he had buckled. I asked the foreman why they had to start work so early and their reasons for suddenly turning their attention to the sanctuary. The answer, as before, was 'orders'.

I had to admire Sloane's cunning and the swiftness with which he had acted. When the congregation arrived I was forced to tell them that there would be no Mass that morning, but that they should come back the next day at six. If we were going to defeat the enemy, we would have to outflank him. However, I knew that a six o'clock start would be impossible for those who relied on buses and that attendance would inevitably be down. Round two in the fight had undoubtedly gone to Sloane. He turned up later in the morning to remonstrate with me again, but I told him to take a running jump and he soon disappeared, all his old smugness back in place and a look of grim determination to go with it.

This day of calamities continued when Julia arrived to tell me that her suspension had indeed gone through. I told her to do her best not to worry and that, as soon as I was able, I would summon a meeting of the governors to consider the

180

situation. I was not optimistic that they would reinstate her, but thought it was worth a try and she seemed moderately cheered by the possibility. As she left, I told her that one advantage of not having to work would be that she would not be too exhausted to attend Mass the next morning at six. She promised to do so and I was encouraged the following day by the number who did manage to defy Sloane's challenge and ensure that the Mass was still well attended. When the builders arrived, I asked them whether they intended to work on Sundays and was told that this was indeed the case. The only difference would be that they wouldn't turn up until nine. Sloane, it was clear, had taken pains to be thorough and once again I was forced to admire his tactics. I therefore rang Drone and gave him the job of putting the word around that the Mass on Sunday would be at seven-thirty, also asking him to provide some altar servers. I then rang Mrs. Moss, who assured me that the choir would be ready to sing. So far, I felt, I was managing to keep one step ahead of my smug friend, but I wondered what other surprises he might have in store for me. It was important to be prepared and I thought long and hard over the next couple of days of stunts he might pull to prevent Sunday's Mass from happening. There had already been a report in the *Echo* about the two 'rival Masses' that would be occurring and I knew that the media would be out in force. Sloane would clearly love to be able to tell them that there was no story and that my Mass had been cancelled, but I saw no way he could bring this about, short of persuading the builders to turn up in the middle of the night.

The dismantling of the old high altar was certainly proceeding apace and I was sad to see the great thing, ugly as it was, come down. The sanctuary was beginning to resemble a bomb-site and I was warned by the foreman that entering it was unsafe. I told him that I did not propose saying Mass with a hard hat underneath my biretta and that I was going to carry on as normal, using the modern stone altar that as yet remained untouched. This was the first time I had been grateful that this second altar had been put in. The builders clearly thought I was mad and told me that, quite literally, any accident that occurred would be on my own head. Their presence meant that my life in the church was now a much more noisy one, but Terry relieved me quite often and I was able to go and have a bath over at his house. Julia and the others also visited frequently and, to a smaller, more select group, I was able to give my next sex and Catholicism talk in the church. Drone popped in whenever he could to discuss the Sunday Mass, proposing that it should be videoed for posterity, and even Spencer White turned up to give me his support. All in all, then, things were building up to quite a climax and I had the feeling that somehow or other this Mass would bring with it some form of closure. I expressed this view on the Friday evening to Julia, who had appeared at the sacristy window just as I was finishing a lonely meal of macaroni cheese and chips. She had brought a bottle of wine with her and, after she had opened it, the conversation turned to what we had achieved with our Forward to the Past policy.

'We've highlighted some important issues,' I said.

'We had no choice.'

'I couldn't just carry on doing things I no longer believed in.'

'Of course not.'

I sipped at the wine, reflecting on the events of the last week, and Julia asked me whether I was any clearer now about what the immediate future would bring.

'Well, I can't go on like this. For a start, its not very comfortable here. The bishop rang me yesterday and asked whether I'd like to go on a course in America at some liturgical institute or other, but I knew the kind of institute he had in mind so told him he could stuff it. Then he asked me whether I thought I would benefit from psychometric testing.'

'What on earth is that?'

'I'm not exactly sure, to be honest. What I do know is that the bishop's always been mad keen on the ability of psychology to solve the world's problems, so probably wants some test results that show I'm as mad as a hatter. That would sort out things very nicely for him. I told him I was quite sane and that all I wanted was to be able to say the traditional Mass in peace.'

Despite my profound scepticism about the bishop's suggestions, they had raised the question once again of what I would do once the present trauma was over. There seemed no easy answer to this and a year in America had for a moment seemed quite tempting. However, I was now determined to leave the parish on my own terms and not be forced into some re-education programme reserved for dissenting priests. I asked Julia whether she had had any further thoughts about her own career.

'Well,' she replied, pouring me another glass. 'I think my best bet is to try and find a school in a diocese that uses *Dogma and Doctrine*. I'll be sorry to leave here because it's where I was brought up, but I don't see any alternative.'

I agreed that this might be the best way forward, refraining from telling her that I thought it unlikely she would find any diocese where our favourite course held sway, such was the dominance of trendy catechists over the school religious curriculum. We finished off the wine and I began to feel relaxed for the first time since my return from France. A kind of calm came over me as if the end of all striving was near, a curious emotion given that it seemed to be entering its most dramatic phase. I thanked Julia again for all the help she had given me and she went on her way, leaving me musing for the umpteenth time on her abundant charms and how, if circumstances had been different, I might have been donning a bow tie myself and doing exactly what Spooner had tried.

On the Saturday evening, Drone and I decided it might be a good idea to have a Holy Hour, during which the Rosary would be recited for the success of the following day's Mass. The word was therefore put round and when the time came people began to drift in in impressive numbers, Terry and the Beast among them. The latter had brought with him his entire extended family. This proved highly alarming as he turned out to have six brothers, all as big as him. As they descended on me in the sacristy at the end of the Holy Hour, I was reminded of the days when, at school, I used to have to face opposition rugby packs.

'Listen, Jim,' said the Beast, pounding me on the shoulder and putting his face disturbingly close to mine. 'I sometimes wonder if you're not a teeny bit naïve.'

I asked him what he meant.

'Don't you see? Sloane isn't a fool. He'll do anything to stop the Mass tomorrow and you've left things wide open for him.'

'How?'

'By leaving the church unguarded. Do you really think those builders will turn up at nine o'clock tomorrow?'

I confessed to him my doubts that they would stick to the advertised timetable and admitted it had crossed my mind that they might turn up earlier.

'It's a racing certainty,' said the Beast, 'which is why I've brought you my brothers.'

The latter now all fixed their gaze on me, evidently intending their collective expression to be reassuring. The result, however, was to make me wonder whether it might not be better to make a hasty retreat while I was still in one piece.

'They're going to stay here all night, Jim. If those builders turn up early, they won't hang around long. Get my drift?'

I got it all right and expressed my gratitude for this excellent plan. I couldn't have been more grateful if the entire Swiss Guard had turned up.

'Right, that's settled, then. The lads will stay here while you and I go off to the pub.'

There was some protest from the brothers at this, but the Beast promised that we would return quite soon and give them a chance to go across the road later. Before I knew it I had been whisked away and was tucking into steak and chips, accompanied by a very welcome pint of Old Fool. This was followed by three or more glasses of the same, after which I gratefully retired to the sacristy where I saw six camp-beds now lined up next to mine. Before the 'lads' had returned from the pub I was asleep.

On waking the next morning, I found them already up and about and congratulating themselves on a job well done. Much to my surprise, my old friend Miller was with them, and it was explained that they had met in the public bar the night before and he had turned up early that morning to lend them a hand. He seemed delighted by the role he had played in the dawn patrol, especially as he had been able to use his dog to good effect.

'The builders turned up, then?' I asked.

There was a good deal of grunting in reply.

'At six,' said Miller. 'They won't be back.'

I expressed my profound gratitude and, after they had all gone off to bring some order to the sanctuary, prepared for Mass. Soon the hordes started to arrive, including the press and TV cameras. There was a small demonstration from the WAR! ladies, led by Buller and Phillips, which included a banner saying 'LIBERATE OUR CHURCH!' and a bit of sporadic hymn singing. I gave a brief interview to the TV people and greeted some of the congregation as they came in. Fortunately, the day was fine and Drone had gone so far as to lay on coaches for those living in more outlying rural areas. Sloane was nowhere to be seen.

The Mass began with a long procession of both servers and choir round the side of the church, starting at the sacristy and entering by the front door. This was all filmed by the TV cameras, while simultaneously being videoed for posterity by a friend of Drone's. As we entered the church, the congregation began to join in lustily with the chant, a very moving moment that helped me remember why I had started my revolution in the first place. Then we progressed onto the now battered-looking sanctuary, covered as it was with scaffolding and building materials. The 'lads' had done a good job cleaning it up, but the overall impression was still that of a building bombed in wartime.

185

Everything during the Mass went splendidly and I delivered what I hoped was a stirring homily, in the course of which I sneaked in a few references to the immemorial nature of the traditional liturgy and how appalling it was that it should no longer be available to the majority of Catholics. Much of this was also filmed by the TV people and I was gratified later on to hear that an excerpt had appeared on the lunchtime news. When the Mass was over I said the customary prayer for the sovereign and we processed out again, to be greeted by a beautiful, bright February morning that lifted my spirits even further. The crowds did not seem to want to depart and I must have spent about an hour and a half talking to people in the car park, all of them urging me to carry on the fight and not be browbeaten by modernists like Sloane. In due course I was able to stagger back, exhausted, to the sacristy for breakfast and ponder what my smug friend would make of it all.

At one o'clock, Mavis Bird appeared with my lunch. Her mood was decidedly agitated.

'I thought I would act as your spy at the eleven o'clock Mass, Father,' she said, laying out the meal.

'What was it like?' I asked.

She pulled a face.

'Terrible. The worst I have ever been to. Mr. Tonks had composed a new Mass setting.'

Somehow, this did not surprise me.

'What did he call it?' I asked.

'*A Mass for Unity*. That silly woman vicar was there, too.'

'Who? Anthea Smith?'

'Yes, the one with the teeth and the dog collar. She gave a sermon.'

I groaned.

'Anything else?'

'The Sisters of Servitude were there.'

'Did they dance?'

'Well, I wouldn't call it dancing, Father, but, yes, they did do a kind of jig during the sermon.'

This sounded even more bizarre than usual, but apparently Anthea Smith had read the sermon very slowly to a musical accompaniment while the sisters had 'interpreted' it. I asked what the sermon had been about.

'I didn't really listen. Something about Oneness and Togetherness, I think.'

Finally, I enquired how many people had been present.

'Quite a few, actually, but I'd never seen most of them before. I think they were from the Minster.'

So, I reflected, Sloane had been reduced to this, an ecumenical service packed with buddies of Anthea Smith to fill up an otherwise half-empty hall.

I thanked Miss Bird for the lunch and, after she had left, decided to have an afternoon snooze, delighted by the way things had gone. At six I staged another Holy Hour, followed by Benediction, after which I invited people to stay on for adoration of the Blessed Sacrament. I eventually shut up shop at eleven and retired to bed, a happy man.

TWENTY-TWO

The fire was already far advanced when I awoke, smoke coming under the door that separated the sacristy from the main body of the church. I opened this and realised I had made a mistake, for the flames were raging fiercely and it was clear I would have to make a pretty snappy exit through the door leading to the car park. In my dressing-gown I rushed across to the presbytery and alerted Sloane, who called for the fire service and then helped me begin a feeble attempt to dowse the flames. It was hopeless. The fire had engulfed the whole of the nave and by the time the engines arrived it was already clear that not much could be done to save the church. When word got round as to what was happening, people gathered from all directions to gaze on the smoking wreck that was Cheeseminster Catholic church. Various theories began to circulate as to the cause of the blaze, some suggesting an electrical fault connected with the building work in the sanctuary, while others were of the opinion that candles lit during the adoration had somehow started the blaze. Drone was convinced that it was all an expression of God's wrath over the reordering, while later I even heard a theory that Sloane had started the fire on the orders of the bishop so that a completely new, super church could be built with the insurance money.

All I knew was that my little rebellion was now at an end. A few days later, I packed my things and headed off to stay with my brother and his wife in Leeds to consider my future. It did not take long to work out what I wanted to do and that's why you are all now getting this letter from the south of France. My visit after Christmas had convinced me that the monastery of Notre Dame-de-Monts would be the perfect place to recuperate after my spell in the trenches and, fortunately for me, the bishop agreed. When I applied to enter the monastery a few weeks later as a postulant the abbot decided to take me on, though before things go much further he wants a full report of exactly what happened in England to judge if I'm likely to be a thorn in his side. I suppose I could give him a copy of this letter, which forms in a way my main defence. Being able to say the traditional Mass everyday in the company of like-minded people of my own age has been like a warm bath after the rigours of life with Sloane, and my French is becoming more proficient by the day. I spend a good deal of time singing Latin psalms in choir with the monks, while the rest of the day is divided between study and manual chores. The weather is now oppressively hot, but I think I could get used to this. Certainly, the place is very beautiful.

As for the church at Cheeseminster, it will not be rebuilt. Owing to the falling numbers of practising Catholics in the diocese and the equal difficulty in finding priests, the bishop has produced a plan to rationalise resources and Terry's church will remain as the only one in the town. Terry himself won't be there, however, because he recently offered to move to Muckford and the bishop agreed to let him go. After the fire, it was Terry who had to say the Sunday Masses in the hall when Sloane finally left, for, as it turned out, no other priest was available. My feeling is that Terry will be much happier festering in a backwater like Muckford and I wish him and his liver well. Canon Taylor, sadly, died in May, leaving instructions in his will for his requiem Mass to be said in the old rite. The Beast performed this service for him, the funeral being attended by practically all the priests in the diocese. I decided to stay away, feeling that England was still a little bit hot for me at present. The Beast has, in fact, now introduced a sung Latin Mass into his own parish on a Sunday without protest from any of the obvious quarters, perhaps wise given his size. He has promised to come over and visit me when he gets the chance.

Julia wrote to me last week and explained that she will be moving in September to a non-Catholic primary school in Gorgehampton. I hope she will be happy there. She tried to find a job in a Catholic school where they use *Dogma and Doctrine*, but it seems I was right about the impossibility of achieving such an aim. She now has a new boyfriend, a member of the CRC who teaches at a Catholic independent school in the area. Her letter was accompanied by notes from the Misses Bird in which they said that Lavender Buller and Miranda Phillips were now going to Mass at the cathedral in Gorgehampton, having been given short shrift by Terry when they tried the usual WAR! antics on him after my departure.

Tonks, meanwhile, deprived of a venue for his musical extravaganzas, apparently intends to have a break from church music and concentrate his energy on getting the Nurdles into the country music charts. The other day he finally sent me the CD of their greatest hits I've been expecting for so long, which I might offer to the abbot for use here as a musical interlude during meals. Knowing their rather peculiar tastes in popular music, it is quite possible the French will take to the Nurdles' unique sound and I have ambitions to open up a whole new market for Tonks at the abbey shop. Drone, meanwhile, has also written to say that the video that was shot of the final Latin Mass has gone down a storm with the hierarchy of the CRC, and there are plans to put it on sale to the members. A kind of posthumous fame might therefore await me in England after all.

I reserve the two most disturbing pieces of news until last. Firstly, it has just been announced that Sloane is to become a bishop, and I wouldn't put it past him to end his career as archbishop of Westminster. His television programme about priests who stray was very well received and his career as a Catholic media spokesman looks assured. I think, on the whole, I am better off in France, at least until Sloane and his like have finally been replaced by a generation that values tradition and doesn't want the Catholic Church to be painlessly absorbed into the Anglican. When that day will come, only Providence knows.

I must finally talk about Spooner. Needless to say, it did not take him long to drive Isobel away for good and I received a letter from her in March telling me it was all over. Apparently, what finally broke the relationship was an evening they spent together that ended up in Spooner's flat. Against her better judgment, Isobel accepted an invitation for 'coffee' and finally saw the squalor in which her boyfriend lived. He then proposed marriage to her again and, when she refused, told her she was fickle and unreliable, launching into an attack on her character that ended with a paean of praise for Julia, the 'only woman I have ever loved.' After this, Isobel told him where he could stick his ring and their relationship with it, resulting in Spooner spending two weeks ringing her up and calling on her in an effort to win her back. In the end, she only managed to get rid of him by putting a block on her phone and threatening to report him to the police for stalking.

Not much later, I heard from Spooner himself. He informed me he had now changed his life completely, so ashamed was he of the way he had treated women, and intended to spend his days atoning for his sins. A few weeks ago he wrote again to say he was coming to France to see if my abbot would accept him as a postulant in the monastery. Ever since then I have been praying that the abbot will take one look at him and send him packing. I do not wish Spooner any ill will, but if he wants to be a monk, let him do it somewhere else. Fortunately, he knows no French, so I think we might see him booking a return flight to England pretty soon.

So there it is. Those of you not of the Faith will probably judge from my account that all Catholics are barking mad and need locking up, an opinion that at times I confess I have shared. It wasn't always like this, though, and one day, perhaps even in my lifetime, sanity may prevail again.